Soda Poppery

The History of
Soft Drinks
in America
SODA POPPERY

with Recipes for Making
& Using Soft Drinks PLUS
Easy Science Experiments

STEPHEN N. TCHUDI

CHARLES SCRIBNER'S SONS · NEW YORK

*For Christopher "Red Head Flapper" Tchudi
and Michael "Klondike Fizz" Tchudi*

Illustration of bottles on p. 11 reproduced from John J. Riley's *A History of the Soft Drink Industry,* 1958, courtesy of the National Soft Drink Association. The trademark "Coca-Cola" is used with the permission of The Coca-Cola Company. Pepsi-Cola logotype and Pepsi Challenge text and illustration reproduced with the permission © of PepsiCo, Inc. Moxie logotype used by permission of The Monarch Company, Atlanta, GA 30341. Beetle Bailey cartoon on p. 44 copyright © 1983 King Features Syndicate. Dr Pepper logotype owned by the Dr Pepper Company; used by permission. Vernors logotype used by permission of the Vernors Company and Union Brands. Yoo-Hoo advertisements used by permission of Yoo-Hoo Chocolate Beverage Corporation. Sugar-Free Hires advertisement on p. 110 courtesy of The Procter & Gamble Company. Shoe cartoon on p. 114 reprinted by permission: Tribune Media Services, Inc.

Copyright © 1986 Stephen N. Tchudi

Library of Congress Cataloging-in-Publication Data

Tchudi, Stephen, 1942–   Soda poppery.
Bibliography: p.   Includes index.
Summary: Presents the history of soft drinks in America, from mineral water to caffeine-free diet soda, and provides recipes and experiments for making and using soft drinks.
1. Soft drink industry—United States—History—Juvenile literature. 2. Carbonated beverages—Experiments—Juvenile literature. [1. Soft drink industry—History. 2. Carbonated beverages]   I. Title.
TP630.T25 1985   338.4'7663'620973   85-40289
ISBN 0-684-18488-5

Charles Scribner's Sons
Macmillan Publishing Company
866 Third Avenue, New York, NY 10022
Collier Macmillan Canada, Inc.

Printed in the United States of America

First Edition

3 5 7 9 11 13 15 17 19 VB 20 18 16 14 12 10 8 6 4 2

Acknowledgments

For their help and suggestions, I am grateful to:

Tee Downes, School of Packaging, Michigan State University

Harry Ellis, Historian and Librarian, the Dr Pepper Company

Barbara Giordano, Yoo-Hoo Chocolate Beverage Corporation

Cheri Lofland, National Soft Drink Association

Philip Mooney, Archivist, the Coca-Cola Company

Edward M. Rider, Corporate Archivist, Procter & Gamble Company

Patricia Steinauer, Consumer Correspondent, Pepsi-Cola U.S.A.

David Toberisky, Charles Scribner's Sons

and especially

Frank N. Potter, "The Moxie Man," Newport News, Virginia.

Contents

Acknowledgments   v
Introduction   ix

PART I: The History of Soft Drinks in America   1

1. Taking to the Waters   3
From Health Spa to Laboratory   7
Artificial Mineral Waters as Medicine   10
Something Extra: Sugar and Flavoring   12
From Soda Fountain to Factory   17
Some Brands That Never Made It   20

2. The Brand-Name Soft Drinks and How They Originated   21
The Honeymoon Drink: Hires' Root Beer   21
The Pause That Refreshes: Coca-Cola   25
Pepsi-Cola Hits the Spot   37
Two Golden Oldies: Moxie and Dr Pepper   40
Two Un-Colas: 7-Up and Canada Dry   50
Summing Up: Vernors and Yoo-Hoo   52

3. The Selling of Soda Pop 57
Gimmicks and Giveaways 58
Celebrity Endorsements 66
Slogans and Jingles 70
Problems and Perplexities 73
  Pure Food and Drugs 74
  Alcoholic Beverages and Prohibition 76
  The World Wars 78

4. The Soft-Drink Wars 83
The Pepsi Challenge 83
Motivational Research and the War for Your Mind 88
The Battle for International Sales 91
A Big Business Grows Bigger 94
Expanding the Soft-Drink Line 96

5. The Present and Future of Soft Drinks 103
Soft Drinks on a Diet 106
  Lo-Cals and No-Cals 106
  Banned in the United States 108
  The Nu Sweetener 111
So Where's the Caffeine? 112
What Next? 116

PART II: Making and Using Soft Drinks 119
Introduction to Part II 121
Brew and Bottle It Yourself 124
The Home Soda Fountain 133
Soft-Drink Recipes 137

Appendix: For Further Information—Addresses 141
Bibliography 143
Index 145

Introduction

Soft drinks—those sweet and fizzy beverages you consume while watching TV, doing homework, playing video games, and relaxing with your friends—soft drinks are at least as American as apple pie. Americans were pioneers in developing the soft-drink industry one hundred years ago, and we consume millions of bottles, cans, and glasses of carbonated beverages every day. Our love of soda pop has spread to other countries as well, and the names of American soft drinks are known all over the globe.

A century ago, most soft drinks were sold in drugstores. They were dispensed at soda fountains, one glass at a time, and the pharmacist would experiment with combinations of flavorings to discover a drink his customers would enjoy. The druggist might even tell people his "tonics" would cure ailments from weak nerves to swollen toes, that soda pop was actually a kind of health food. Today the drugstore soda fountain is virtually a relic of the past, and soft drinks are bottled by machine. To prevent false claims, the government looks over manufacturers' shoulders to make certain they're selling exactly what's being advertised.

The history of soda pop is awash with legends and rumors about the ingredients in carbonated beverages and what they will do to you. It has been said that if you drop a nail into a bottle of pop, the nail will dissolve. (If that's right, what happens in your stomach after you've consumed a soda?) There are stories about horrible things people have found inside bottles of pop: mice, rats, bugs. (If those claims are true, are there impurities in soda that you *can't* see?) Some people claim soft drinks contain narcotics; others believe the sugar in pop makes you hyperactive; still others argue that the recipes for soft drinks are so secret that hardly anyone knows what's really inside a can or bottle of pop, not even the government.

This is a book about Soda Poppery—the facts and myths and legends and science and history of the All-American soft drink. As you read, you'll discover when soft drinks were invented and how they became popular. You'll learn the stories of our most popular brands and what's in their secret recipes. You'll read about some odd and peculiar soft drinks of yesteryear, and you'll come to know what makes pop "pop" and how much sugar there is in "sweetwater." You'll discover how to make soft drinks at home and see recipes that use soda pop in such curious ways as a holiday ham glaze and the liquid in a cake.

From time to time as you read you'll find some sections marked:

---

* IDEAS & EXPERIMENTS *

Each of these projects will suggest ways to extend your knowledge beyond the pages of this book. There's one to get you started on the opposite page.

There are a great many soda-pop hobbyists in the world, people who are fascinated by the history of soft drinks or collect things related to

* IDEAS & EXPERIMENTS 1 *

Begin keeping a notebook or scrapbook about soft drinks. You can use a looseleaf or spiral-bound notebook as a place to record your ideas and observations about soda and to save items you collect. Here are some ideas for a Soda Poppery notebook:

—Interview some of your friends about their favorite soft drinks. What are their preferred brands? Why do they choose to drink particular brands?

—Keep your notebook close to the TV for a week and make notes on commercials for soft drinks. What brands advertise most frequently? Do the ads discuss flavor? health? fun? price? What do your observations tell you about soft-drink advertising today?

—Look through current magazines and newspapers for soda-pop ads. Clip and paste these into your notebook, adding your observations about how the soft-drink companies go about selling their products.

the soft-drink industry: bottles, bottle caps, advertisements, articles of clothing with brand names printed on them. As you explore the IDEAS & EXPERIMENTS of this book, you may discover that you have a new hobby: Soda Poppery.

PART I

The History of Soft Drinks in America

Chapter 1

Taking to the Waters

Soda.
Pop.
Soft drink.
Tonic.
Sweetwater.
Carbonated beverage.
Fizzwater.

Soft drinks are called by many different names in different parts of the country. But whether you call your carbonated drink *pop* or *soda* or something else, its name tells you something about how soft drinks originated and became popular.

For example, many New Englanders use the name *tonic* when they ask for a soft drink. Webster's *Collegiate Dictionary* defines "tonic" as "an agent (as a drug) that increases body tone . . . one that invigorates, restores, refreshes, or stimulates." Webster's also says that a tonic may be a "liquid medicinal preparation." A tonic, then, sounds more like medicine than something you'd drink for pleasure.

3

As it turns out, carbonated beverages had their start as medical cures.

If you look back in history to the times of the Greeks and Romans about two thousand years ago, you won't find any record of soda pop, but you will find that people believed *water* to be a good cure for much of what might go wrong with the human body. The Greeks and Romans used hot baths, cold baths, and steam baths to treat illnesses and to provide relaxation for weary bones and muscles. The Greek physician Hippocrates, whose pledge of service to humankind is still recited by doctors, praised the curative properties of water. A natural spring on the Greek Mount Helicon was called "The Hippocrene," and its waters were said to have the power to inspire poets.

In other parts of the world, from China to Egypt to Turkey to North and South America, healers have used baths and waters to cure their patients. Today athletes sit in steam rooms or whirlpool baths to relax stiff joints and muscles. Patients suffering from diseases and injuries ranging from arthritis to broken bones take *hydro-* (or water-) therapy. Water, then, still has a good reputation as a tonic for sick or injured bodies.

---

* IDEAS & EXPERIMENTS 2 *

Look up "Health Clubs" in your telephone yellow or white pages. How many of them advertise the use of water as a part of their exercise or therapy programs? Do they have swimming pools, Jacuzzis, whirlpools, or steam rooms? You might want to telephone the spa and ask a few questions about what they think the water does to help people. Write your observations in your Soda Poppery notebook.

Hundreds of years after the Greek and Roman empires had fallen,

Europeans discovered natural springs in places like Vichy and Pyrmont in France. Some of these springs flowed hot because of volcanic action deep in the earth. Others gave forth waters with strong tastes and odors from dissolved chemicals and minerals. The waters were said to be good tonics. From the 1300s on, it was common for wealthy Europeans to "take to the waters," to head for health "spas" where they would soak in the springs and even drink the water, no matter how bad it tasted or smelled. These spas were legendary for curing such diseases as rheumatism (stiffness of the joints), gout (swelling of toes, ankles, and knees), nephritis (kidney infection), and dyspepsia (indigestion). Modern scientists have argued that many of these cures may have been due simply to a change of diet or daily routine: people may have gotten better at the health springs just because they had left dirty, crowded cities or were just taking time off and resting. Nevertheless, the reputations of the health spas grew.

---

* IDEAS & EXPERIMENTS 3 *

Many Americans have become concerned about the purity of water that comes from the tap and chemicals that may have been added to it. Thus they choose to drink bottled water. Go to your local supermarket or health-food store and study the different brands of waters that are available. You might even buy a small bottle of naturally carbonated spring water. (Perrier is one of the most popular brands.) Drink some and savor the taste. As you do, you become part of a tradition that goes back hundreds of years.

Among the most popular of the spa waters were some that bubbled and fizzed naturally. At first, no one knew where the bubbles came from. People spoke mysteriously of *spiritus mineralis*—"the spirit of the mineral waters"—or *spiritus sylvestris*—"the wild spirit" of the waters. Eventually scientists learned that the water contained a particular kind of gas—*gas carbonum*—or what we know as carbon dioxide, and the waters were said to be "carbonated." They discovered that when carbon dioxide is trapped in the earth it can dissolve in water. When that water reaches the surface—say, in a spring—the carbon dioxide bubbles out naturally, just the way your soft drink starts to fizz when you snap off the cap.

In the United States, the most famous natural carbonated waters were found at Saratoga Springs in upstate New York. These waters had been known to the Mohawk Indians long before white men came to the region. The Indians called them "Medicine Waters of the Great Spirit." Many prominent Americans visited the springs at Saratoga for rest and cures, including the first president, George Washington.

A doctor of colonial times inspected the waters and wrote:

The medicinal waters . . . are brisk and sparkling like champagne. In drinking, they strike the nose and palate like bottled cider, and slightly affect the head of some people by their inebriating quality.

It is not likely that the carbonated waters actually inebriated people, but it is evident that those who consumed them felt curiously refreshed and believed their ailments had been cured.

In the late 1700s and early 1800s, enterprising businessmen in both Europe and America realized that the waters could be bottled and sold to those people who couldn't make the long trip directly to a health spa. Saratoga waters thus appeared in bottles with such brand-name labels as Vichy (after the famous springs in France), Star, Selzer, High Rock, Lincoln, Chief, Victoria, and Carlsbad. The bottled waters were consumed as cures for fever, nausea, indigestion, and dehydration. In fact, so much water was drawn from the Saratoga Springs that the water level dropped dangerously, and the state of New York had to pass laws limiting consumption.

From Health Spa to Laboratory

Almost from the time the natural spring waters were discovered, their "magical" powers intrigued scientists, who tried to duplicate the waters in their laboratories. The scientists were able to create artificial sulfur water (foul-smelling and bad-tasting) that was thought to be as healthful as nature's own. They learned that if they dissolved chalk in a solution of weak acid, they could create bubbling water, which they claimed was "stronger and more energetic than the same Waters when issuing from the laboratories of nature." Carbonated water, the scientists discovered, could be made from such interesting ingredients as oil of vitriol and alkali or carbonate of soda and vinegar (from which we get the name "soda"). They wrote papers on "Factious Airs" to deliver to scientific societies and invented names for the gas that bubbled from their laboratory vessels: *cretacious acid, aerial acid.*

A British scientist, Joseph Priestley, is generally given credit for being the first to tame carbon dioxide, or what he called "fixed" air. He went to a brewery and managed to collect some carbon dioxide given off by beer as it fermented. (See IDEAS & EXPERIMENTS 4 for an explanation of how carbon dioxide is produced through fermentation.) When he bubbled the gas through water, some of the gas dissolved, giving an "aciduated" taste—a tang quite like the spa waters. In 1772 Priestley published a book with the imposing title:

DIRECTIONS FOR IMPREGNATING WATER WITH FIXED AIR; IN ORDER TO COMMUNICATE TO IT THE PECULIAR SPIRIT AND VIRTUES OF PYRMONT WATER, AND OTHER MINERAL WATERS OF A SIMILAR NATURE.

He had created a carbonated beverage, something quite like our modern club soda. Preistley also conducted experiments that showed that the "fixed air" in this water could be absorbed into the human bloodstream, where it would combine with mild acids. He had discovered why carbonated waters can bring relief to the sufferer of an "acid stomach" by neutralizing acidity.

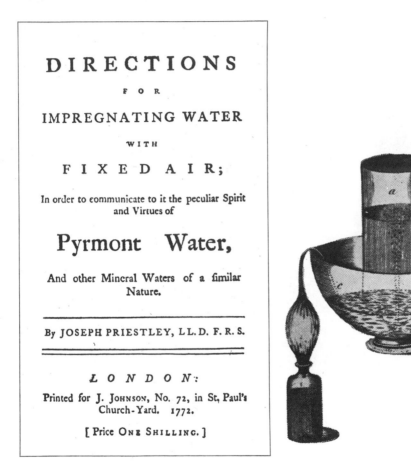

Joseph Priestley's pamphlet on carbonated water
and his laboratory apparatus for collecting carbon dioxide

* IDEAS & EXPERIMENTS 4 *

There are two ways you can create carbon dioxide at home; both duplicate methods that have been known to chemists and cooks for hundreds of years.

Method #1. Look about your kitchen and find some bicarbonate of soda (sometimes called baking soda). Put a teaspoon in a glass and stir it into water. Then add two teaspoons of vinegar and watch the mixture bubble. The bubbles are carbon dioxide (written as CO_2 in chemical shorthand). They are released when a carbonate (the baking soda) is treated with an acid (vinegar). This same method is used to make biscuits or pancakes rise; carbon dioxide is released from baking powder, which is a combination of baking soda and an acid.

Method #2. Place about three teaspoons of sugar in a glass of lukewarm (about 110°F) water and dissolve it. Then add a pinch of dry active yeast and place the glass in a sunny or warm spot for several hours. When you come back, you'll see bubbles bursting at the surface. This is a process of fermentation in which the yeast grows by feeding on the sugar. The reaction produces carbon dioxide as a by-product. Cooks also use this combination of ingredients to make bread rise. We'll employ the yeast method in Part II of this book as we show you how to brew your own soda pop at home.

Scientists now know that carbon dioxide in water creates a weak solution of carbonic acid, which has some disinfectant properties. It may be that in Joseph Priestley's time, carbonating water helped to purify it, thus adding to the health-protecting properties of soda waters.

Artificial Mineral Waters as Medicine

Soon after Joseph Priestley's experiments, industrialists began producing mineral waters commercially and bottling them. In 1781, Thomas Henry of Manchester, England, sold bottles of what he called a "Mephetic Julep" that he claimed was an "efficacious . . . grateful medicine" in curing "putrid fevers, scurvy, dysentery, bilious vomitings, hectic, etc." Sick people purchased his Julep in large quantities.

   In London, Jacob Schweppe, a financier, founded Schweppe and Company to bottle artificial mineral waters. The British government considered Jacob Schweppe's waters a medicine, not a pleasure drink, and to his annoyance they charged three pence per bottle extra as a medical tax. You can still find soft drinks sold under the name

Schweppe, and "Schweppervescence" has become an advertising slogan for the Schweppe line of carbonated beverages.

On American shores, Benjamin Silliman, a chemistry professor at Yale University, in New Haven, Connecticut, was one of the first to sell artificial mineral waters. By 1807 he had perfected ways to dissolve carbon dioxide in water, but he had another difficulty: the bottles he used would often break under the pressure created by the gas. To help people like Silliman, bottle manufacturers experimented with different sizes and shapes and explored various ways of sealing bottles with cork

Soda-water bottles from the 1800s

and wire. When the bottles were opened, they made a small explosion, which gives us yet another name for carbonated beverages: as Robert Southey, a British poet, explained, soda was called "pop" because "pop goes the cork when it is drawn."

The weak bottles also created a problem for the workers who did the bottling and corking. Bottles often exploded, especially in warm weather, and many people were injured by flying glass. As progress was made in developing stronger soda-water bottles, the way was prepared for the popularization of soft drinks for home consumption.

But remember, Benjamin Silliman, the Yale chemist, was not selling soda pop. He was a chemist trying to help the ill, not a purveyor of pleasure drinks. He advertised that his soda waters would cure sour stomach, heartburn, poor appetite, and headache.

Apparently people in nineteenth-century America bought a fair share of soda water—enough, at least, for one book, Putnam's *Handbook of Useful Arts,* to warn that overuse of mineral waters "would sometimes be attended by mischievous results, especially if indulged in to the extent to which some persons pursue the use of soda water." We have to suppose that then, as now, the drinking of too much pop, too fast, created an upset stomach.

Something Extra: Sugar and Flavoring

Up through 1850, artificially carbonated waters were rather bland. If you've ever sipped plain club soda, you know that it fizzes and has a "bright" taste, but that's about all. It required the addition of flavorings and sugar to bring about soft drinks as we know them.

At first, the flavorings in soda pop grew from medical uses. Pharmacists added roots and herbs to carbonated waters, not to make them taste better, but to improve their curative properties. They soaked raspberry leaves, ribwort, nettles, birch bark, currant leaves, dandelion, sassafras, and strawberry leaves in soda water. In the process, they discovered that the soda water came to taste better (though by our current standards, not a great deal better).

In addition, Americans had long known how to make nonalcoholic "small beer" by brewing molasses or sugar along with roots, yeast, and herbs. The colonists were encouraged to avoid drunkenness by consuming small beer or "Switchel" (made from molasses, vinegar, and ginger brewed with yeast in water). These brews were strong stuff and

---

* IDEAS & EXPERIMENTS 6 *

Years ago, an expert on the tastes and flavors of soft drinks wrote:

> The flavor of a ginger ale is the resultant of the sensations attributable to the sweet taste of the sugar or other sweetening agent, the sour taste of the acidulant [the acid], the pungent taste of the ginger, the taste and odor of the other flavoring components, the tickling sensation caused by the impingement of the bubbles of carbon dioxide gas against the walls and roof of the mouth and tongue, the sensation of coldness due to the low temperature of the beverage, the body effect of the sugar, and finally the feeling of satisfaction given by a good soft drink.

His language is a bit fancier than ours, but his is a careful description of the taste sensation of a soft drink. Open a can or bottle of your favorite pop. Sip it. Savor the taste. Feel the "body," or syrupiness, of the drink. Then in a page of your Soda Poppery notebook, write a description of "the feeling of satisfaction given by a good soft drink."

---

probably wouldn't be much to our liking, but they were sweeter than plain soda water, and thus they helped in making *sweetwater* part of an American tradition.

Often this sweetwater was made in large vats or kettles in the farmhouse kitchen. Mrs. Isabella Beeton's *Book of Household Management*, written in 1861, told how to make ginger ale from sugar, ginger root, cream of tartar, lemons, and yeast. The mixture was set to brew by the fire overnight, then bottled and corked.

GINGER BEER.

INGREDIENTS.—2½ lbs. of loaf sugar, 1¼ oz. of bruised ginger, 1 oz. of cream of tartar, the rind and juice of 2 lemons, 3 gallons of boiling water, 2 large tablespoonfuls of thick and fresh brewer's yeast.

Mode.—Peel the lemons, squeeze the juice, strain it, and put the peel and juice into a large earthen pan, with the bruised ginger, cream of tartar, and loaf sugar. Pour over these ingredients 3 gallons of *boiling* water; let it stand until just warm, when add the yeast, which should be thick and perfectly fresh. Stir the contents of the pan well, and let them remain near the fire all night, covering the pan over with a cloth. The next day skim off the yeast, and pour the liquor carefully into another vessel, leaving the sediment; then bottle immediately, and tie the corks down, and in 3 days the ginger beer will be fit for use. For some tastes, the above proportion of sugar may be found rather too large, when it may be diminished; but the beer will not keep so long good.

Average cost for this quantity, 2s.; or ⅓d. per bottle.

Sufficient to fill 4 dozen ginger-beer bottles.

Seasonable.—This should be made during the summer months.

Isabella Beeton's recipe for ginger beer

Many farmhouse cooks developed their own recipes for small beers and ales using any roots and herbs that were available. They might use dandelions dug from the yard, black birch bark stripped from a newly felled tree, or sassafras or sarsaparilla roots pulled from a flower garden. Among the most popular beverages was "root" beer, concocted from the plant roots a cook could find. Thus the root beer of yesteryear tasted much different from that we drink today. It was stronger, more like medicine, and its taste varied from one home or farm to another, even from one batch to another.

As you can see from Mrs. Beeton's recipe, home brewing was a considerable amount of toil and trouble. It is not surprising that people began to look for easier ways to get their soda waters. In larger towns and cities, soda pop came to be sold by the glass in local pharmacy shops. Practical devices were invented to create carbonated waters from a soda "fountain." One inventor, John Matthews, sold a machine that would create soda water using ground marble (a source of carbonate) and sulphuric acid. His entire apparatus—including a carbon dioxide generator, frame, fountain spigot, soda glasses, marble, and sulphuric acid—sold for $195.78. That was a great deal of money in the 1800s, but the public interest in soda pop was so great that many pharmacists could afford the machinery.

The druggists began experimenting to create new soda fountain flavors. Orange and lemon juice could easily be added to carbonated water to improve flavor. (In Europe and England today "limonade" is a name applied to all soft drinks, since in the early days soda waters were often lemon flavored.) Some of the druggists were also chemists, and they worked on creating artificial flavors and colors in their laboratories. They discovered that caramel (which is made from burnt sugar) colored carbonated water a rich brown, and to this day caramel is one of the principal coloring ingredients used in colas. (Read the label on a can of cola to confirm this.) They learned how to create synthetic vanilla flavoring and used that to make "cream" soda.

By the year 1890, the development of chemical flavors had become so sophisticated that the Tufts Company of Boston could offer druggists the following:

Almond	Blood Orange	Chocolate
Banana	Calisay	Coffee
Blackberry	Catawba	Crabapple
Birch Beer	Celery	Cranberry

Tufts also had mixes for special combination drinks or flavors:

| Ginger Ale | Kola Champagne | Violet |
| Limeade | Pepsin Soda | Walnut Cream |

Do you wonder what Walnut Cream tasted like? You will find a recipe for it in Part II.

Some of the flavorings, like lemon, were made from natural ingredients. Others involved laboratory re-creations of natural products (it's cheaper to create *vanillin* in a laboratory than to squeeze it out of vanilla beans). However, many flavorings turned out to be chemicals that fool the tongue and taste buds. Chemists discovered that the following combination of chemicals tastes surprisingly like strawberries:

Amyl nitrate, benzyl acetate, ethyl acetate, ethyl butyrate, methyl salicylate, ethyl benzoate, nerolin, amyl fomate, and cinnamon oil.

Raspberry flavoring could be made from a combination of chemical acetates, fomates, and benzoates with some vanillin and other ingredients tossed into the pot.

Many of these artificial flavorings were colorless, and druggists decided to add dyes or coloring to make their soft drinks resemble the natural color of the fruits or plants they tasted like. Therefore chemically flavored cherry soda would be dyed red; lemon-lime would be tinted yellow or green.

An era had begun. If you look on the label of most soft drinks today, you'll discover that seldom are fruit drinks made from real fruit, and seldom are the flavors real extracts or essences. What you get in a modern soft drink is chemical flavoring and dye in sugared or artificially sweetened carbonated water. In our time, the federal government has become very concerned about these chemicals, fearing that some of them may produce cancer or other diseases. At the turn of the century, however, prior to the passage of the Pure Food and Drug Act, pharmacists were free to experiment with any dye or flavoring that caught their imagination.

Some druggists went beyond mixing flavors in carbonated water. One pharmacist added milk to strawberry, pineapple, vanilla, and carbonated water to create what he called a Moorish Sherbet. And it was only a matter of time before someone began adding ice cream to soda water to create the immortal ice cream soda.

All in all, the 1800s must have been an exciting era for soda poppers. If you went to the drug store, you might find the druggist serving an exotic new flavor or trying out a secret recipe. Soft drinks became so popular that people expected them to be served in public places. In his novel, *The House of the Seven Gables,* Nathaniel Hawthorne reported a scene in which patrons of a tavern were *not* served their favorite soft drinks:

No less than five persons, during the forenoon, inquired for ginger beer or root beer or any kind of a similar beverage, and obtaining nothing of the kind, went off in exceedingly bad humor.

From Soda Fountain to Factory

It became a national pastime for Americans to go to their local soda fountain and have the druggist make a soda right on the spot in a favorite flavor, say, checkerberry or catawba. As soft drinks became more popular, the soda fountain equipment to make them became more elaborate. In 1861, Gustavus Dows of Lowell, Massachusetts, patented a fountain that won a medal at the Great International Exhibition in Paris. His machine included a coil of tubing that snaked through ice to cool the carbonated water, containers for various kinds of syrup, a place where ice was shaved into "snow" to be placed in drinking glasses, and fancy pumps and faucets to control the flow of soda water. An ornate soda fountain amazed visitors to the Philadelphia Exposition in 1876.

Elaborate soda fountain shown at the Philadelphia Exposition of 1876

As popular as the drugstore soda fountain may have been, however, it was not always convenient, for a person wanting a cool soft drink on a hot summer day had to go to the pharmacy to get one. If you lived in a rural area, you might be miles away from a refreshing pause. Manufacturers and salespeople realized this and thus worked at new ways of bottling their product to make it portable.

You'll recall that in 1807, Benjamin Silliman complained that his bottles broke under pressure in warm weather. Fifty years later, Mrs. Beeton's recipe for ginger ale warned users to tie in the corks of the bottles securely, because fizzy soft drinks had a habit of blowing corks right out of the bottle.

Inventors had explored and tried to patent some 1,500 different kinds of stoppering devices for hundreds of different kinds of bottles. Eventually, stronger bottles, made by machine rather than produced one at a time by a glass blower, became standard, and in 1892, William Painter patented a "crown cap," which is essentially the same as the kind found on soda bottles until the recent development of the twist-off cap. Bottling soda pop became more reliable and safer.

All of these technological developments paved the way for bottling soft drinks for home consumption. By the end of the 1800s, bottling plants had sprung up all over America, each making its own brand of pop, often with favorite flavors that had been invented by the local pharmacist (who sometimes quit the drugstore business to become a full-time soda-pop bottler). Many of the factories were small, because the bottling and capping still had to be done one bottle at a time, and most of the brands were distributed just a few miles from where they were bottled.

A very few local brands became so popular they spread all over the country; you'll read about them in the next chapter. Many of the local brands, however, were produced for just a few years. It is with regret, then, that we list the following wonderful-sounding soft drinks that have fallen by the wayside.

Some Brands That Never Made It

Little Daisy

Imperial Nerve Tonic

Klondike Fizz

Ironbrew

The Dutchess

Grapine

Ho-Ko

Cycla-Phate

Delaware Punch

Grape Julep

Cherry Blossoms

Cherry Julep

Orange Whistle

Charleston Pop

Ten Pins

Old Eagle's Punch

Longabero

Star "Wishniak"

Virginia Rambler Nectar

Buffalo Mead

Fillipin Fizz

Kolafra

Tangerette

Bongo Beer

Bull Ginger Ale

Lime Phosfizz

Celery Cola

Grapine

Grape Mist

Tempo-Wyne

Bluebird

Egyptian Mystery

Red Head Flapper

Brule's Juices

Pilgrim Ginger Ale

Smile-O

Bludwine

Orange Glory

Chapter 2

The Brand-Name Soft Drinks and How They Originated

You can't go into the store today and buy a bottle of Red Head Flapper or Klondike Fizz. However, in most parts of the country you *can* buy soda pop named Coca-Cola, Hires, Dr Pepper, Canada Dry, and 7-Up. Many of the brands we drink were created in the 1800s and have survived to our time. Through a combination of interesting flavor and skillful marketing, plus a drop or two of good luck, certain brands became established as national favorites. In this chapter, you'll learn the stories of their beginnings.

The Honeymoon Drink: Hires' Root Beer

As you've read, root beer is a beverage that traces its roots all the way back to colonial days, when farmers' wives brewed it at home. For people who didn't want to go to the trouble of digging their own roots, a few pharmacies in the 1800s began to market packets of roots and herbs for brew-it-yourself root beer. It was a Philadelphia, Pennsylvania, pharmacist, Charles E. Hires, who made a brand-name business of it.

In 1870, while on his honeymoon, Hires spent time experimenting with root beer recipes. He discovered what he regarded as an especially tasty combination made with sixteen roots, herbs, and berries, including such ingredients as juniper, pipsissewa, spikenard, wintergreen, sarsaparilla, hops, vanilla beans, ginger, licorice, deer tongue (a plant, not tongues from real deer), dog grass (also a plant), and birch bark. (You have to wonder what Mr. Hires's new bride was doing all the time he was experimenting with this concoction.) He named this drink Hires' Root Tea and marketed packets of the ingredients back in Philadelphia. His friends liked the drink, but they suggested that more people might buy it if it had a robust name like Hires' Root *Beer*.

Mr. Hires continued to experiment, and by 1876 he had created a mix of herbs and roots that not only made good root beer, but also dissolved more easily in water than some other mixtures. The packet sold for twenty-five cents, and when brewed with water, yeast, and sugar, it yielded five gallons of root beer—or about one-half cent for a twelve-ounce glass.

That same year, 1876, the United States celebrated its one-hundredth birthday with a huge exposition in Philadelphia. Charles Hires rented a booth at the exposition and let people sample his root beer while he sold packets of the mix. He received such an enthusiastic response that he began advertising and selling his "powders" by mail. In 1884 he took out a small ad in a national publication, *Harper's Magazine,* informing people about his "delicious, sparkling, and wholesome beverage."

Charles Hires also developed a liquid extract of his powders to make home brewing even easier. But he realized that the future of soda pop did not lie with home-brewed drinks. He saw that people preferred the convenience of soda fountains and, even more important, they liked the ease of take-home bottles. Thus in 1893 he began bottling Hires'

Root Beer and selling it in the Philadelphia area. He stepped up his advertising campaign to a national scale, and just a few years later he was selling three million bottles per year and buying full-page ads in magazines like *Ladies' Home Journal.*

Harper's Magazine *ad for Hires' Root Beer*

An 1897 ad showed that Charles Hires was trying to sell to two basic markets: the home-brewer and the person on the go. A child—the famous Hires' Root Beer boy—was shown holding a package of root beer extract in his right hand and a bottle of the soft drink in his left. Regarding the extract, the ad declared, "There is more fun than trouble in making it." However, if a person was "awheel," "journeying on a train," or "dining at the hotel or cafe," then "a bottle of this delicious beverage" would "make you feel at home." Mr. Hires also reminded readers of the drugstore tradition for soft drinks by stressing that his product had "health giving properties":

> Soothing to the nerves, vitalizing to the blood, refreshing to the brain, beneficial in every way.

Hires claimed his root beer:

> gives children the strength to resist the enervating effects of the heat, bridges the convalescent over the trying part of a hot day, helps even a cynic see the brighter side of life.

These claims were based on the reputation of time-honored herbal cures and the fact that some of the basic root beer ingredients were respected as home medicines: juniper berries were supposed to be good for kidney troubles; dog grass was a diuretic that could rid the body of excess fluids.

Hires had unquestionably overstated the value of his root beer. It was precisely that sort of advertising claim that caused the U.S. government to check the assertions of soft-drink makers about what their products could accomplish. As you'll discover later in this book, however, modern soft drinks carry some inflated claims of their own.

During the last decade of the 1800s, Charles Hires's "root tea" went on to establish itself as the nation's most popular root beer, and it is a brand that is still manufactured today. In the 1960s, the Hires company experienced a decline in sales when the U.S. Food and Drug Administration declared that sassafras, a major flavoring ingredient of root beer, might cause cancer in laboratory animals and could no longer be used for flavoring. Hires lost a big share of the soft-drink market while its chemists looked about for other ways to create a good root beer flavor.

Today the Hires Company is owned by Procter & Gamble of Cincinnati, Ohio, a conglomerate that sells everything from laundry detergent to toothpaste. In a recent advertising campaign, Procter & Gamble has reminded consumers of the Hires history by labeling its product Hires' *Original* Root Beer. That, in itself, is a somewhat misleading claim, since the modern Hires isn't at all like Charles Hires's original tea or the soda he sold at the 1876 exposition. Nevertheless, the name is still original, and soda poppers should know that Hires is just about the oldest of the nationally prominent soft drinks.

Incidentally, the Hires Company continued to make its liquid extract for homemade root beer until 1983, when sales had declined to the point that the product was taken off the market. Now, if you want to make root beer at home, you may just have to do it the way our ancestors and Charles Hires did it: digging up roots, soaking them, then mixing them with water, sugar, and yeast. You'll learn how to do this in Part II, where we'll also show you a shortcut recipe for Mock Root Beer.

The Pause That Refreshes: Coca-Cola

In the early 1880s, a number of soft-drink makers were experimenting with the ingredients from two plants: the coca shrub, which is found in South America, and the cola (or kola) tree, from Brazil and the West Indies. Coca leaves contain compounds called "alkaloids," including traces of the narcotic, cocaine. Cola seeds, which are about the size of a chestnut, contain caffeine, the pepper-upper that is also found in tea and coffee. As early as 1881, drugstore soda fountain operators had created and sold drinks using these ingredients, including:

Imperial Inca Cola	Coca-Coffee	Coca-Malta
French Wine Coca	Burgundia Coca	Cocafeine
Kola Phosphate		

One of the experimenters was John S. Pemberton of Atlanta, Georgia. Born in 1833, Pemberton had served in the Civil War as a cavalry soldier. Then he became a creative pharmacist, inventing such products as Globe of Flower Cough Syrup, Indian Queen Hair Dye, Triplex Liver Pills, and Extract of Styllinger (the last of these intended to improve one's blood). Like Charles Hires, Pemberton was first and foremost a medicine man, not a soda popper. The name of his company, founded in 1885, was Pemberton Chemical Company.

One of John Pemberton's drugstore remedies was French Wine Coca, an "Ideal Nerve Tonic and Stimulant," made with wine and coca leaves. Some of his teetotaling customers wouldn't buy it because of the wine, so he began to search for a nonalcoholic drink that would have the same effects.

According to legend, John Pemberton brewed his medicinal syrups in a three-legged pot over a fire in his back yard. Starting with the recipe for French Wine Coca, he eliminated the wine and added some cola extract to get caffeine into his brew. Because cola (and caffeine) have a bitter taste, he sweetened the mixture with sugar and then added lemon oil. Dr. Pemberton believed that this combination of ingredients would relieve tiredness, give a lift to the spirits, and cure dyspepsia (or upset stomach). Finally, the story goes, he carried his syrup down to Jacobs' Drug Store in Atlanta and suggested that the druggist, Willis Venable, try some out on the customers.

Venable dispensed the mixture at the soda fountain, putting a teaspoonful into a glass of plain water. Folks liked the taste of the new medicine and thought it might be good for their health.

Then, some stories say, Willis Venable accidentally mixed some of the syrup with carbonated water at the fountain. Other versions of the

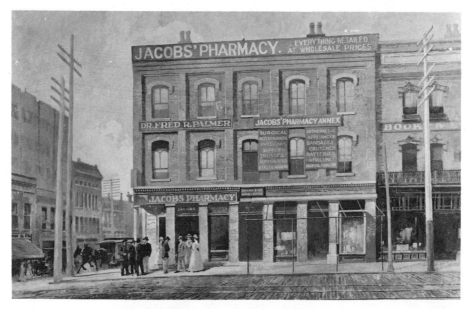

Jacobs' Pharmacy in Atlanta, Georgia,
where Coca-Cola was first served in 1866

story suggest that a customer proposed adding fizzwater to improve the taste and to make the new drink a better cure for stomach ailments. In either case, a magic combination of ingredients came together at Jacobs' Pharmacy: coca, cola, and carbonated water. The drink John Pemberton had created might have been intended as medicine, but he invented a "pause that refreshes," which lead to the giant of the soft-drink industry: The Coca-Cola Company.

Credit for the name of the new drink is generally given to Frank Robinson, bookkeeper for Pemberton Chemical Company. Robinson not only suggested the name, but took out his pen and roughed out a design for the new product's insignia (or logotype). His drawing was refined and eventually became the world famous Coca-Cola logotype:

Coca-Cola logotype

Everything was in place in 1886—the ingredients, the name, and the logo. However, Coca-Cola did not do a flood of business right off. During the first year, Willis Venable only sold about thirteen glasses of the new drink a day. A year later, perhaps discouraged by the slow sales, John Pemberton sold the Coca-Cola recipe and brand name to another Atlanta druggist, Asa Candler.

It was Mr. Candler who, as "sole proprietor" of the drink, put Coca-Cola on the soda-pop map. He was a skilled marketing man, always

An advertisement showing Asa G. Candler as sole proprietor of Coca-Cola looking for new ways to advertise Coca-Cola. He gave away fans, calendars, clocks, and even urns and jars, all with Frank Robinson's logotype on them. Mr. Candler doesn't seem to have been certain whether he had bought the rights to a soft drink or a medicine. An 1891 calendar stressed that Coca-Cola was "a delightful summer or winter drink" but also said that it was a good cure "for headache or tired feeling." On the same calendar, Candler included an ad for De-Lec-Ta-Lave tooth medicine, which would supposedly whiten teeth, cure bleeding gums, and "neutralize acidity of saliva."

About this time Asa Candler made another marketing decision that was to influence Coca-Cola's rise to national prominence. Here again, we have to rely on legend, but stories claim that an unknown man approached Candler and said that for either $5,000 or $50,000 (both amounts are mentioned in versions of the story), he would tell Candler how to become rich with Coca-Cola. Mr. Candler is said to have paid the man, who gave him a slip of paper with just two words on it: "BOTTLE IT."

Whether or not that story is true, we know that Asa Candler followed the lead of Charles Hires and decided to offer Coca-Cola for sale by the bottle. As happened with Hires' Root Beer in bottles, Asa Candler's sales of Coca-Cola increased dramatically.

About this time, too, Candler figured out a new way to handle the bottling process. He felt it would be too expensive to bottle Coca-Cola in Atlanta, then ship it all over the country. Soft drinks are mostly water, and water is both heavy and expensive to ship. He created what is called the "franchise" bottling system, in which he licensed bottling plants in different locations. The first Coca-Cola franchise opened in Vicksburg, Mississippi, using syrup prepared in Atlanta, but adding carbonated water there on the spot. The franchises were sold so rapidly and were so successful that by 1895, Asa Candler could claim that "Coca-Cola is now drunk in every state and territory in the United States."

There has always been a great deal of secrecy surrounding the recipe
for Coca-Cola syrup. One story tells that Asa Candler hired Frank
Robinson, the bookkeeper, away from Pemberton Chemical Company
because he knew the secrets of Coca-Cola. It's said that Frank Robinson could simply sniff a batch of syrup and tell whether it had been
made according to the formula. He could also allegedly sip the cola
drinks of competitors and tell what ingredients they used. Thus he,
along with Asa Candler, became the keeper of the secret recipe.

Howard Candler, Asa's son, reports that the formula and ingredients for Coca-Cola syrup were kept behind a fireproof, sheet-iron
door, locked with a combination known only to Asa Candler and Frank
Robinson. Asa Candler wrote all the purchase orders for ingredients
himself, so no employees could know what was being bought. When
the various oils, seeds, and leaves arrived, Asa Candler logged them in
personally and hand-carried them to the laboratory, where he used

A calendar advertising Coca-Cola

The Brand-Name Soft Drinks

two giant "percolators" to create what he called "the coca and cola tincture," a "brilliant light brown fluid with a biting taste."

When Asa Candler was about to retire, he called Howard to him and taught him to brew this secret "tincture." Howard Candler later wrote:

> I was initiated into the secrets of the product which have been passed down by word of mouth to the most trusted employees. . . . The total number of persons who have known the secret formula since Dr. Pemberton's day can be added up on the fingers of one hand.

Howard remembered the day he learned the formula:

> One of the proudest moments of my life came when my father . . . initiated me into the mysteries . . . inducting me as it were into the "Holy of Holies." No written memorandum was permitted. No written formulae were shown. Containers of ingredients, from which the labels had been removed, were identified only by sign, smell, and remembering where each was put on the shelf when it came from the supplier or was made in the same locked room. To be safe, Father stood by me several times while I compounded the distinctive flavors to see that proper quantities were used of the right ingredients and in the correct order to insure the integrity of the batches and to satisfy himself that his youthful son had learned his lesson and could be depended upon.

Although competitors have tried to discover the formula, it has remained a Coca-Cola company secret. Mostly. In 1917, the courts told Coca-Cola to reveal its formula as a way of proving its claim for a trademark. In case you've ever wondered what is in a Coke, here's what the Company told a judge in Chattanooga, Tennessee. Coca-Cola's formula, the "Holy of Holies," was revealed as:

Caffeine (grains per fluid ounce)	0.92-1.30
Phosphoric acid (H_3PO_4) (percent)	0.26-0.30
Sugar, total (percent)	48.86-58.00
Alcohol (percent by volume)	0.90-1.27
Caramel, Glycerine, Lime Juice, Essential Oils, Plant Extractives	Present
Water (percent)	34.00-41.00

So what is Coke? The simplest answer is that (in 1917) it was about half water and half sugar, plus small quantities of other ingredients. Phosphoric acid was added to give the drink a bit of zip or bite. Alcohol was present mainly as a solvent for the essential oils and plant extractives (just as many flavorings you can buy at the store today are based in alcohol). Caramel, as you may recall from the last chapter, is a coloring made from burnt sugar; glyccrine was added to give the beverage "body," to make it just a bit thicker than water. As you can see, Coca-Cola varied in composition, with differing amounts of water, sugar, and other ingredients. When people nowadays talk about the "better" flavor of "old" Coca-Cola, they are not referring to a single, consistent flavor.

But as you can also see, The Coca-Cola Company did not have to reveal the crucial details of its formula. Just what were those "essential oils" and "plant extractives"? The secret of Asa and Howard Candler was not revealed in Chatanooga.

The traditional recipe for Coca-Cola is still a carefully guarded secret. Philip Mooney, the archivist and historian of The Coca-Cola Company explains:

Only a small number of people know the precise way in which all the ingredients combine to form the syrup that is the basis for the finished product. The Coca-Cola Company goes to great lengths to protect the security of the formula and to ensure that it will remain a secret. The formula is maintained in a vault of the Trust Company of Georgia.

However, modern scientists have set to work analyzing the ingredients of cola drinks. A good guess as to the essential formula of most colas is:

Ingredient	Dissolved in 9 Gallons of Alcohol
Extract of coca leaves	2.0 drams*
Neroli oil	6.0 drams
Lime oil	8 ounces
Sweet orange oil	14 ounces
Nutmeg oil	2.5 ounces
Cassia oil	5.0 ounces
Lemon oil	28.0 ounces
Vanilla extract	28.0 ounces

*A dram is 3.888 grams, about ⅛ ounce.

That's a huge recipe for cola tincture, enough to create flavorings for thousands of gallons of cola drinks. It is interesting, because there is very little *coca* in it. There is *no* cola in this recipe, and The Coca-Cola Company was once taken to court for false advertising on the grounds that it didn't use any cola nut derivative in its drink. The real taste of cola drinks (as you can see) comes from lemon oil and vanilla extract. (In Part II, we'll show you a recipe for Mock Cola using these same basic ingredients.)

At the turn of the century, Coca-Cola's instant success spawned a great many imitators. Some manufacturers chose a similar name; others used a similar logotype; still others tried to imitate the secret formula. *Fortune Magazine* once called these imitators "serpents in the garden" and quoted Asa Candler as saying:

. . . unscrupulous pirates often found in even the most respectable trade positions find it more profitable to imitate and substitute on the public than to honestly avail themselves of the profit and pleasure which is ever the reward of fair dealing and competition.

A commission established by the president of the United States in 1908 found that the cola drinks being manufactured in the country included, in addition to Coca-Cola:

Afri Cola	Lime Cola	Charcola
Ala Cola	Lime Ola	Cherry Kola
Carre Cola	Nerve Ola	Cola Soda
Celery Cola	Revive Ola	Field's Cola
Chan Ola	Rocola	French Cola
Chero-Cola	Rye Ola	Jacob's Cola
Cola-Coke	Standard Cola	Kola Creme
Cream Cola	Tokola	Kola Vena
Four Cola	Vani Kola	Loco Kola
Hayo Cola	Wise Ola	Mintola
Heck's Cola	Cirtro Cola	Ro-Cola
Kay Ola	Kike Ola	Schelhorn's Cola
Kola Ade	Lon Kola	Vine Cola
Kola Kola	Mexicola	Kola Pepsin Celery
Kola Phos	Pau Pau Cola	Wine Tonic
Kos-Kola	Pepsi-Cola	

Not all of these brands were either deliberate or accidental imitations of Coca-Cola, but a brand with a name like Cola-Coke seemed very suspiciously close.

Asa Candler had registered the name Coca-Cola with the U.S. Patent Office in 1893, and from then on the stockholders in his company urged him to take legal action "against parties who are selling substitutes for, or imitations of, Coca-Cola." Over the years, the Company filed law suits against soda pop companies selling:

Coke-Ola	Coca & Cola	Ko-Kola
Kola Koke	Coak	Co Kola
Kos-Kola	Kaw-Kola	Cola Soda
Cola-Coke	Koko Kola	Klu-Ko
Chero-Cola	Hava-Kola	

---

* IDEAS & EXPERIMENTS 8 *

Now that you know something of the Coca-Cola formula, drink a Coke and test your taste buds. Can you detect the lemon? the vanilla? In recent years, Coke has branched out to offer sugar-free and caffeine-free versions. Obviously, each of those new pops deviates from the original John Pemberton formula. Taste test all three versions. Can you detect taste differences? Try this experiment with your friends to see if they can tell the differences.

The most intense legal battle, however, was waged with another Atlanta company that called itself the Koke Company. This law suit went all the way to the United States Supreme Court, where it was settled by the famous American judge, Oliver Wendell Holmes. He said that Coca-Cola had become unique:

The name now characterizes a beverage to be had at almost any soda fountain. It means a single thing coming from a single source, well known to the community.

He ruled in favor of Coca-Cola and ordered the Koke Company to change its name. Thus when The Coca-Cola Company advertises today that "Coke is IT!," they mean, among other things, that Coca-Cola is a unique drink, despite its imitators.

In April 1985, on the eve of Coca-Cola's one-hundredth birthday, the Company made a startling announcement: *it was changing the formula of Coca-Cola.* Although Coke sales were still number one, the lead over Pepsi had declined, and company executives decided to tamper with the "Holy of Holies." The old formula, called Merchandise 7X, would remain locked in the bank vault, and a new one, Merchandise 7X-100, would take a place alongside it. The new formula was discovered while Coke scientists were experimenting with a diet cola, and was described by the Company as "smoother and rounder." Most experts agreed that the new formula is *sweeter* than old Coke, perhaps an acknowledgment of the American sweet tooth.

Some Coke fans were enraged by the change and went to the stores to buy all the old Coke they could find. Other fans said they liked the new taste better, that Coke was still "IT." People calling themselves the "Old Coke Drinkers" actually took the Company to court to get it to restore the original formula.

In July 1985, only two months after introducing the new Coke, The Coca-Cola Company announced that it was bringing back the original formula under the name "Classic Coke." The Company had obviously underrated consumer loyalty to the flavor discovered by John Pemberton ninety-nine years earlier, and "old" Coca-Cola is unquestionably the classic of the soft-drink industry.

Pepsi-Cola Hits the Spot

The story of Pepsi-Cola is surprisingly similar to that of Coke. While Coca-Cola was created by a Georgia pharmacist in 1886, Pepsi was invented by a North Carolina druggist just a few years later, in 1890.

Caleb D. Bradham was owner of a drugstore in New Bern, North Carolina. He was said to be very popular with his customers, a chatty fellow who liked to "tend bar" at the store and to concoct new flavors of soft drinks for his friends. Bradham also read the pharmaceutical journals, which described soft-drink recipes as well as new medicines. In 1890 he was experimenting with a coca and cola mixture that he named Brad's Drink after himself. He also purchased the trademark and name for a rival soft drink, Pep-Kola. After several years of experimentation he settled on a recipe and a name, Pepsi-Cola, for his fountain creation. The original Pepsi trademark was registered with the U.S. Patent Office on June 16, 1903.

The original Pepsi-Cola logotype

You can see that the Pepsi logo, with its swirling print, was quite similar to Coca-Cola's. It seems safe to suppose Mr. Bradham knew of the competing drink that had been so successful in Atlanta. In fact, you might say that Mr. Bradham's imitation of Coke—the taste, the name, the logotype—was the first real Pepsi Challenge. The two drinks have been fierce competitors ever since. Coke has taken Pepsi to court on several occasions for alleged infringement of its patents and trademarks, though never successfully. There's no doubt that the Coke people regarded the Pepsi crowd as some of the "serpents in the garden" to which *Fortune Magazine* had referred.

One of the most famous battles between the two companies took place in the early 1930s, after both were firmly established as national brands. It started with Mr. Charles Guth, who was not a soda popper at all, but president of a chain of candy stores, Loft's. He sold soft drinks by the glass in his stores, and up through 1930, Coca-Cola had been his brand. In that year, Loft's sold 31,558 gallons of Coke syrup, and Mr. Guth felt he ought to be given a discount price. The Coke people said no.

Angered, Charles Guth *bought* the Pepsi-Cola Company, which was experiencing financial problems, and Loft's Candy Stores began selling Pepsi.

Now Coca-Cola was angry. The company sent "agents" into Loft's stores and had them ask for a glass of Coke. "Coke" was by then protected as a trademark, even though the term had slipped into general language use as a word for just about any cola drink. The agents said that on 620 occasions they were served Pepsi-Cola when they had asked for Coke, and they took the matter to court. The claim was never substantiated, but it heightened the rivalry between the two companies, so that even today, they challenge one another in their advertising.

In 1985, when Coke announced it was changing its formula, Pepsi

---

* IDEAS & EXPERIMENTS 9 *

Collect Coke and Pepsi ads from newspapers and magazines and paste them in your notebook. Compare the ads for the two products on TV and make notes. What claims does each company make for its product? Do they mention one another by name or claim that one tastes better than the other? Which company seems more aggressive in taking on its rival?

celebrated, and employees at world headquarters in Purchase, New York, were given a day off. When public outrage forced Coke to reintroduce its "classic" flavor, the Pepsi people gloated, joking about Coke as "the cola of the month club." Some analysts even believe that before too long Pepsi will achieve its goal of more than ninety years: to outsell Coca-Cola—new or classic—and become the number-one soft drink in the world.

Two Golden Oldies: Moxie and Dr Pepper

Cola drinks—mostly Coca-Cola and Pepsi-Cola—have dominated the soft-drink market in the United States almost since pop was first bottled. However, several other soft drinks invented in the 1800s have survived to our time. Two of these brands, Moxie and Dr Pepper, have not only lasted, but at one time or another actually challenged the big two for supremacy.

Moxie is a dark, caramel-colored drink that looks like a cola but tastes *very* different. It may be that you've never seen or tasted a bottle of Moxie, because in recent years it has been a relatively small competitor in the soft-drink market. You just don't see Moxie in many stores. However, you have probably heard an expression like, "She has plenty of *moxie*," meaning plenty of spunk or vigor or nerve. That word is directly related to the soft drink.

Like many sodas, Moxie was first created as a medicine, not a pleasure drink, and its origins will sound familiar to you, now that you've read about pharmacists John Pemberton, Caleb Bradham, and Charles Hires.

Moxie's creator, Augustin Thompson, was born in Union, Maine, in 1835, and like the other three men, served in the Civil War in the 1860s. Perhaps on account of the suffering he had seen in the war,

Thompson decided to become a doctor. Once he completed his medical studies, he settled in Lowell, Massachusetts.

In 1876, before either Coke or Pepsi had been created, but about the time Charles Hires was experimenting with root beer, Augustin Thompson brewed up a mixture of gentian root extract and other ingredients and called it Moxie Nerve Food. This elixir, he said, "Contains not a drop of Medicine, Poison, Stimulant, or Alcohol."

It was brewed from "a simple sugarcane-like plant grown near the Equator and farther south, [which] was lately accidentally discovered by Lieut. Moxie." Thompson said that Moxie elixir:

> has proved itself to be the only harmless nerve food known that can recover brain and nervous exhaustion; loss of manhood, imbecility and helplessness. It has recovered paralysis, softening of the brain, locomotor ataxia, and insanity when caused by nervous exhaustion. It gives a durable solid strength, makes you eat voraciously; takes away the tired, sleepy, listless feeling like magic, removes fatigue from mental and physical overwork at once, will not interfere with action of vegetable medicines.

How's that for a set of claims? If only Moxie Nerve Food worked as well as its label claimed, human problems would have diminished a hundredfold. Of course, one has to be suspicious of these claims from the start, if only because *there was no Lieutenant Moxie;* he was an invention, like Moxie Nerve Food, of Dr. Augustin Thompson.

Gentian root, the principal ingredient, was not "lately . . . discovered," either. Frank N. Potter, author of *The Moxie Mystique,* traces its use back to the legendary king Gentius of Illyria (Greece) in 61 B.C. Gentius was supposedly cured of his ailments by the root that now bears his name, and he lived to be eighty-seven years old.

Gentian root extract is extremely bitter. Dr. Thompson added sugar to his mixture to make it taste better. The exact formula of original

Moxie Nerve Food is not known, but the drink included chinchona (from the bark of a South American tree; it contained quinine, a cure for fever), sassafras (a major ingredient in root beer and valued for the curative properties of its tea), caramel (for coloring), and other flavorings.

As happened with Coca-Cola, Moxie Nerve Food evolved into a soft drink. By 1884 Dr. Thompson was selling it both as a syrup for drugstore fountains and in bottles. Frank Potter supposes that Dr. Thompson promoted Moxie as a soft drink, in part, because people would drink whole bottles of it, rather than consuming it by the spoonful. Thus they would buy more of it.

Even as a soft drink, however, Moxie had a strong, medicinal taste. It was unlike any soft drink on the market, and for years people had divided opinions about it: some swore by Moxie and would drink nothing else; others thought it was bad-tasting stuff and would never voluntarily let it pass their lips.

Label from Moxie Fountain Syrup

Like Coke, Moxie had a number of imitators, and soon there were many products that looked, tasted, or were named like Moxie, drinks called Proxie, No-Tox, Noxie Nerve Tonic, Noxall, Modox, Rixie, and Toxie. The name Moxie became and still is a trademark, but just as the word "coke" (written with a small "c") came to stand for all cola drinks, "moxie" (with a small "m") passed into the language as a general word for something else.

Frank Potter reports that the name Moxie may have originally been selected by Augustin Thompson because it was American Indian in origin and may have reminded customers about Indian medicine men and their cures of barks and herbs. However, as the medical values of Moxie Nerve food were promoted, the word came simply to mean "nerve," and eventually, to quote Frank Potter, it became a name for:

the spirit of America . . . a word for the audacity of the movers and shakers who continue to change the world.

Moxie has left its mark on soft-drink language in another way. In New England, where Moxie was created and where it enjoyed its greatest sales, soft drinks are still called "tonics." Although Moxie can't claim full credit, there can be little doubt that the popularity of Moxie Nerve Food helped keep alive the wishful idea that soft drinks can be a tonic for better health.

---

* IDEAS & EXPERIMENTS 10 *

Interview people of several generations—older and younger—and ask what the word "moxie" means to them. Have them illustrate it by describing a person who seems to have moxie. Do they have a sense of its meaning as "nervy"? Also ask if any people know the origin of the word. How many people nowadays know of Moxie soft drink? Are they mostly of your generation or an older one?

Moxie in cartoons

In 1906, when the government passed a Pure Food and Drug Act, Moxie dropped Nerve Food from its name, because one couldn't prove that anything in those bottles actually did "feed" the nerves. Moxie was and still is simply a soda pop. It became enormously popular in the United States during the 1920s. The few Moxie drinkers still left take pride in its different taste. The word "moxie" has even been applied to the drink itself: it has been said that it takes plenty of moxie to drink Moxie.

After World War II, sales of Moxie declined. Americans didn't seem to be as fond of a soft drink that tasted like medicine. In 1968, the Moxie Company left New England and bought the Monarch soft drink company of Atlanta, manufacturers of a number of soda pops. The company executives decided to "redesign" the taste of Moxie, making it sweeter and more pleasurable to the modern drinker. But old-time Moxie drinkers said it just wasn't Moxie anymore, and in New England, especially, sales fell even more. The company then switched back to an earlier recipe for its "tonic," closer to Dr. Thompson's original recipe. Unfortunately, Moxie just doesn't have the moxie of yesteryear, either in taste or sales, but it's good to know that this golden oldie of soft drinks, a true American original, is still around today.

From its name alone you might suppose that Dr Pepper has a background in common with that of Pepsi, Hires, Moxie, and Coke, and Dr Pepper did begin as a drugstore medicine, sold as a "tonic, brain food, and exhilarant" in a Waco, Texas, pharmacy. The Dr Pepper story has some interesting twists, though, including a tale of unfulfilled love.

Dr Pepper, King of Beverages

The drugstore of Dr. Kenneth Pepper in Rural Retreat, Virginia

In the early 1880s, a young man named Wade Morrison was employed as a pharmacist's assistant in Rural Retreat, Virginia. Young Wade developed a crush on the daughter of his employer, but the store owner decided the assistant was too old for his daughter and too young to think seriously about marriage. He encouraged Morrison to head out west to seek his fortune, and Wade hit the trail for Texas, ending his courtship of the boss's daughter. The name of the father/boss/store owner was Dr. Kenneth Pepper.

Wade Morrison first moved to Austin, Texas, where he found employment at Tobin Drug Store. When the owners opened a second store in Round Rock, Texas, he was sent there to head up the operation. (In Round Rock, by the way, he witnessed a famous Texas shoot-

The Old Corner Drug Store in Waco, Texas, birthplace of Dr Pepper

out in which the Texas Rangers caught an infamous bank robber, Sam Bass.) Eventually Wade settled down in Waco, Texas, where he became a partner and eventually the sole owner of the Old Corner Drug Store.

You might suppose that this story is leading up to Wade Morrison's inventing a new soft drink, but in fact it was Charles Alderton, a clerk in the drugstore, who experimented with new flavors and discovered a combination that customers especially liked. It was dark, like a cola, but had a rich cherry taste. At this point, Wade Morrison, now a store owner on his own, stepped in and suggested naming the drink Dr. Pepper, after the father of his lost love. Records in the U.S. Patent Office show that Dr. Pepper was first named and served on December 1, 1885.

An early ad for Dr Pepper

Legend has it that Wade Morrison then went back to Virginia, told the girl and Dr. Kenneth Pepper about the new drink, and won her hand and father's approval. The less romantic fact is that Wade never went back to Virginia and he eventually found a bride in Texas.

Like Pepsi, Coke, and the others, Dr Pepper soon became too popular for simple dispensing in drugstore soda fountains. Wade Morrison teamed up with R. S. Lazenby, who was selling Circle "A" brand ginger ale, and the two went into partnership selling both beverages. Soon Dr Pepper became a national brand.

From the beginning Wade Morrison stressed that Dr Pepper was not a cola and did not contain caffeine. Despite the "peppy" sound of the name, Dr Pepper was advertised as standing "alone on the bridge defending your children against an army of caffeine doped beverages." At the same time, the ads said Dr Pepper "brightens the mind and clears the brain; and if you have important business to transact, requiring a clear, cool head and deliberate judgment, drink Dr. Pepper." Other claims for the beverage included curing nervousness and sleeplessness, creating a youthful feeling, correcting stomach ailments, curing a hangover, and providing an "antidote" from excess cigarette smoking.

After the Pure Food and Drug Act of 1906, the Dr Pepper people had to modify those claims, but even today their ads hint that Dr Pepper is a pepper-upper. "I'm a Pepper," says a young, trim, athletic

Dr Pepper logotype

49 *The Brand-Name Soft Drinks*

dancer in a television commercial. "He's a Pepper," the dancer continues, pointing to an equally trim and vigorous pal. "She's a Pepper," he says of a lithe, perky girl. "Wouldn't you," he asks, turning to the audience, "like to be a Pepper, too?" What's being promised? Nothing *specific* (like a cure for nervousness or an antidote to alcohol or nicotine). Nevertheless, it's clear that as in the good old days, manufacturers like to imply that their soft drinks bring about physical well-being.

There's a footnote to the Dr Pepper story that has to do with punctuation. You may have noticed that we haven't always put a period after the *Dr* of Dr Pepper. In the early days, a period was used (you can see it in the older ads and logotype). In modern ads and the current logo, the period is gone; nor is it used in any of the company's publications. Harry E. Ellis, the historian and archivist for Dr Pepper, explains that this change took place in 1960, when advertising people decided that the period cluttered up the logo.

Modern Dr Pepper logotype (without the period)

Two Un-Colas: 7-Up and Canada Dry

7-Up was a relative latecomer in the soda-pop business. It was invented in 1928, some forty years after Coke, Pepsi, and many of the other national brands. Like those drinks, it first came onto the market as a cure for something: in this case, stomach ailments. Unlike the other drinks, however, its creator, C. L. Grigg, was neither a pharmacist nor a doctor. He was a successful seller of soft drinks in the St. Louis, Missouri, area, having had good luck with an orange drink called Howdy. In the late 1920s he ran into some difficulty because several states had ruled that any drink called "orange" had to contain real orange juice rather than artificial flavors. That created problems because bottlers found it difficult to include real orange juice without having spoilage. Rather than re-invent Howdy, Mr. Grigg looked around for a new drink to sell. He created a lemon-lime mixture using artificial flavorings. It was a *lithiated* drink, meaning that it contained some of the chemical, lithium, a widely used cure for depression. The new pop was also highly carbonated, giving it more fizz than the usual soft drink. He named this concoction—brace yourself: Bib-Label Lithiated Lemon-Lime Soda. Can you imagine walking into a store and asking for a bottle of that, or even Bib-Label or Lithiated Lemon-Lime for short? Neither, apparently, could C. L. Grigg, and before long the name was changed to 7-Up.

Because of its extra fizz, its mild lemon-lime flavor, and its lithiated content, 7-Up was advertised as a cure for an upset stomach. "Takes the Ouch Out of a Grouch," read one of its advertisements. Other ads claimed that 7-Up was the best cure for a hangover; it could relieve the upset stomach and headache of a person who had consumed too much alcohol the night before.

Like Dr Pepper, 7-Up didn't contain caffeine. In Chapter 5 you'll read about how 7-Up used its caffeine-free history to launch an advertising campaign as an "un-cola," an alternative to Coke and Pepsi. Now it's interesting to learn the story of another famous brand of pop that never had caffeine and never will: Canada Dry Ginger Ale.

"Down from Canada came tales of a wonderful beverage," read an ad for Canada Dry in the 1920s. This soft drink began its history in the late 1880s, in Toronto, Canada. John J. McLaughlin had experimented with a number of ginger ales. He had sold McLaughlin's Belfast Style Ginger Ale, a heavy, dark brown pop, and McLaughlin's Pale

Dry Ginger Ale, a lighter drink in both flavor and color. McLaughlin found that Canadians preferred the pale dry variety, and soon he began to export it to the United States under the name Canada Dry.

The new ginger ale was expensive—it cost a great deal to ship it down from Toronto. Canada Dry sold for thirty-five cents a bottle, while all the soft drinks made in America were selling for a nickel. Thus it acquired a reputation as a luxury drink for the wealthy. Canada Dry was also used chiefly as a mixer with alcoholic drinks to create a highball. In 1929, when the United States was gripped by an economic depression, Canada Dry sales fell off. People were having a hard time coming up with a nickel for a bottle of Coke or Pepsi, much less thirty-five cents for Canada Dry Ginger Ale.

At that point, the company decided it could lower costs by bottling in the United States, using the kind of franchise system created by Asa Candler of Coca-Cola. "The champagne of ginger ales" became competitive in price with other American drinks and became the best-selling ginger ale. The company also expanded its line of products to include club soda and quinine water (sometimes called "tonic"), among other beverages.

There is an ironic ending to the story of this unique Canadian drink. A few years ago, Canada Dry was sold to a United States company: Dr Pepper. The only thing Canadian about the drink now is its name. The creator of Dr Pepper, Wade Morrison, first got his drink publicized nationally only after he formed a partnership with R. S. Lazenby, who was selling Circle "A" Ginger Ale. By acquiring Canada Dry, the Dr Pepper Company came full circle.

Summing Up: Vernors and Yoo-Hoo

Vernors?
Yoo-Hoo?
To many readers, these names will be unfamiliar.

Are they soft drinks?

Both are regional brands: Vernors in the Detroit, Michigan, area; Yoo-Hoo in the New York/New Jersey region. Although neither of these drinks is a famous national brand, each helps to illustrate the moxie and inventiveness of American soft-drink creators. Each one is a model, in miniature, of the history of American soda pops.

Vernors Ginger Ale was the creation of yet another nineteenth-century Civil War veteran, James Vernor. According to legend, in 1861 James left his home in Detroit to fight in the war. Before departing, he sealed some roots, herbs, and water in an oak cask. After he returned safely from the war, he opened the keg and used the solution to make a unique ginger ale, stronger and darker than a "pale dry" variety (like Canada Dry). Vernors was sold at drugstores, then bottled. Mr. Vernor's son was given the recipe and, through marketing skill, established his drink as a Detroit favorite.

The One Of A Kind Soft Drink

Vernors logotype

Even today the Vernors company follows the recipe of James Vernor, although its equipment is automated and the soda pop is produced in huge quantities. Twenty different ingredients are used to make Vernors. They are processed into a syrup that, the company says, is stored in oaken kegs for four years, just like James Vernor's original batch.

The taste of Vernors is unique. People seem either to love or hate Vernors' strong taste. The flavor is even considered spicy enough by local cooks to be used for basting Christmas turkeys and Easter hams. Recently Vernors has been bought by Union Brands, who announced plans to market this Detroit curiosity all over the country.

Like Vernors, Yoo-Hoo is a drink with a unique flavor that caught on, at least with some soft-drink lovers.

In the 1920s, Mr. Natale Olivieri of New Jersey was bottling Tru-Fruit soft drinks, made from processing fresh fruit. He became skilled at the difficult process of bottling a true fruit drink that did not spoil on grocery-store shelves.

At one point he conceived the idea of a *chocolate* soda pop. Right away there were problems. He learned that in order to bottle chocolate pop, he had to add so many chemicals and preservatives that the flavor was spoiled.

One day, while helping his wife can some homemade tomato sauce, Nate Olivieri began thinking about heat processing, something that wasn't ordinarily done with soft drinks. His wife prepared six bottles

Yoo-Hoo Chocolate Drink

of chocolate pop, using the same process she had for the sauce. Three of the bottles spoiled, but three remained good, and Mr. Olivieri figured he was on to something. He perfected the method of preserving through heat and began to market his drink. He called it Yoo-Hoo because other companies in his area were naming their soft drinks things like Whoopie and Vigor. Those two competitors are long gone, but Yoo-Hoo, "the chocolate action drink," is still going strong around New York.

Yoo-Hoo is a drink that has been more or less adopted by a baseball team, the New York Yankees. During the years that the Yankees were regularly winning the American League pennant and the World Series,

New York Yankee soft drinkers
Left to right: Mickey Mantle, Bill "Moose" Skowron, Whitey Ford,
Elston Howard, Yogi Berra

many of its stars endorsed Yoo-Hoo. The list includes Mickey Mantle, Bill Skowron, Elston Howard, Clete Boyer, and Yogi Berra. By associating itself with these athletes, Yoo-Hoo seems to promise what so many American soft drinks have pledged through the years: strength, health, vigor, vitality, and All-American get-up-and-go.

---

* IDEAS & EXPERIMENTS 11 *

In this survey of major brands and their origins, I may have missed one of your favorites. Some national brands are relatively new—Mountain Dew and Mr. PiBB, for example. Others, like Royal Crown, have very long histories (it started out in the good old days as Chero-Cola). If you are interested in learning the origins of your favorite brand (or some locally distributed brands like Cott in New England or Barqs in Arizona), write a letter to the public relations department of that company. You'll find some addresses in the appendix of this book. You can also check your telephone book for the number of a local distributor, who can supply you with the needed address. When you write, also ask for a copy of the most recent annual report of the company, which will give you some information on how your favorite brand is faring in the bubbly business of soft drinks.

Chapter 3

The Selling of Soda Pop

By the year 1900, Americans were drinking an average of twelve bottles and glasses of soft drinks per year, a dozen for every man, woman, and child in the country. Soda pop was clearly something Americans wanted and enjoyed. Hires, Coke, Pepsi, Dr Pepper, and others were going strong in almost every part of the country, marketed by over 2,700 soft-drink bottlers.

Although the manufacturers took advertising pride in "secret" recipes and formulae, the fact is that by 1900, scientists knew pretty much what was in all soft drinks. In a book with the long and impressive title, *Beverages and Their Adulteration—Origin, Composition, Manufacture, of Natural, Fermented, Distilled, Alkaloidal and Fruit Juices,* Harvey Wiley described and analyzed the chemical composition of every kind of soft drink from ginger ales to root beers to colas. Because most soft drinks used artificial flavors, anyone could buy those flavorings from a supply house. Any bottler could thus produce a drink that was just as flavorful as that of the competition.

In the eighty-plus years that have passed since 1900, very little has happened to change the uniformity of soft drinks. Despite claims for uniqueness, most pops consumed today are made from similar ingredients. The taste differences between, say Pepsi, Coke, and other colas, are not very great, and there are few significant differences between Hires' Root Beer and other national and regional brands of root beer.

One amazing thing has changed since 1900: per person consumption of soda pop has risen from twelve bottles per year to 359 in 1980. Think about that figure—359—for a moment. Americans drink just about one bottle or can of pop per person per day, and that average includes people (like babies) who don't drink any soda at all. There has been a thirty-fold increase in soft drink consumption since 1900.

What accounts for this extraordinary rise? One answer is that Americans have simply come to drink more and more soda pops because they enjoy them so much. However, a better explanation has to do with the ways the soft-drink manufacturers have marketed their products. Where the 1800s can be said to be the age of the *invention* of soft drinks, the 1900s—our century—is the era of the *selling of soda pop.*

Gimmicks and Giveaways

Early in the game, soda poppers offered free souvenirs, trinkets, and prizes to their customers. They gave away tickets to ball games, hats, rulers, pencils, book covers, aprons, banners, napkins, clocks, matches, cigarette lighters, door plates, pocket knives, watch fobs, decals, mirrors, and umbrellas. Soda-pop drinkers have received drinking glasses, calendars, bumper stickers, shirt buttons, sewing kits, picture frames, erasers, playing cards, sweatshirts, scarves, and key chains. All these gifts have sported the logotype of the soft-drink company doing the giving.

Advertisers have also wanted grocery and pharmacy owners to display their products, so they have given away cardboard cutouts and displays, outdoor and indoor signs, thermometers, serving trays, special glasses for soda fountain use, and even Tiffany lampshades. Many of these items, like the customer giveaways, have become valuable "collectables."

Coca-Cola school supplies and giveaways

Dr Pepper serving tray

59   *The Selling of Soda Pop*

The Coca-Cola Company estimates that in the first ninety years of its history (1886–1976), it spent over seven hundred *million* dollars on advertising and promoting its product. With inflating advertising costs and increasing competitiveness in the soft-drink industry, vast fortunes have been spent by Coca-Cola since then. Coke's longtime position as number one in the soft-drink industry is in no small measure due to its willingness to advertise and promote its beverage.

Other manufacturers have spent small and large fortunes on ways of bringing their product to the attention of the public. Pepsi-Cola, for example, has hired airplane skywriters to spell out the name of its product in puffs of smoke in a blue sky; Canada Dry has hot-air balloons embossed with its logo; and more than once soda-pop manufacturers have hired the Goodyear Blimp to advertise their wares.

1894   1899–1902   1900 ———— 1916   1915

The evolution of the Coca-Cola bottle

1894 and 1899-1902: *Hutchinson-style bottles with wire fasteners to hold in corks.* 1900-1916: *bottles designed for crown-cap seals, with a diamond-shaped label added.* 1915: *the original "ribbed" or "contour" bottle designed by Mr. Samuelson of the Root Glass Works.*

Soda poppers have also felt a need to keep their products looking unique. Coca-Cola, with its many imitators, determined early in this century to create a different kind of soda bottle. As one Coke executive put it, the company wanted a bottle so special that a customer would recognize its shape *even in the dark.* Coca-Cola took this idea to the Root Glass Company of Terre Haute, Indiana, and turned the problem over to one of its specialists, a Mr. Samuelson. Legend has it that he went to the *Encyclopaedia Britannica* and made a sketch of a cola nut, then designed a bottle with bulging sides that resembled it. You can check the encyclopedia yourself to see whether a Coke bottle looks like a cola nut. In any event, Mr. Samuelson's bottle, introduced in 1915, became one of the most famous packages in marketing history: the "ribbed" or "contour" green glass Coke bottle.

| 1923 | 1937 | 1957 | 1961 | 1975 |

The evolution of the Coca-Cola bottle
1923 and 1937: *slight variations on the contour bottle, which allowed Coca-Cola to renew its patent.* 1957: *contour bottle with Coke label printed rather than embossed.* 1961: *no deposit/no return bottle.* 1975: *plastic contour bottle with a twist-off cap.*

For years Coke was available only in this bottle, which contained six and one-half ounces of soda. Buyers probably *could* recognize it by feel in the dark. Eventually, Coke found it had to offer its product in different sizes—twelve-ounce, sixteen-ounce, quart, liter bottles—and in cans as well as bottles. In fact, Coca-Cola doesn't even make the six and one-half-ounce bottle any longer, which makes it a real collector's item. Nevertheless, you can still see the "cola nut" bottle at your local supermarket, available in a variety of sizes. Incidentally, the shape of that bottle was sufficiently unique for Coke to register it with the U.S. Patent Office in 1960.

The Dr Pepper Company has also created some unusual bottles as a way of promoting sales. There is nothing special about the shape of its commemorative bottles, which are straight-sided soft-drink bottles, but each one is embossed with the date of a special event: a football game in Dr Pepper's home state of Texas, the U.S. bicentennial celebration of 1976. Over twenty-five of these bottles have been produced, and they, too, are collector's items.

Dr Pepper commemorative bottles

The Moxie bottle was plain, too, but because of Moxie's success, it was often imitated. Early in this century the company published advertising brochures urging its customers not to accept look-alike bottles. To help publicize the appearance of original Moxie bottles, the company had some large models—over eight feet high—constructed and carried around in trucks. The biggest Moxie bottle of them all, however, was over thirty-five feet high. It was built at Pine Island Amusement Park, near Manchester, New Hampshire, and was used as a stand where free samples of Moxie were provided.

The giant Moxie bottle

The Moxie Company was a pioneer in creating novelty advertising campaigns. It used a fleet of fifty-four gasoline, steam, and electric automobiles to visit over 40,000 American towns and cities early in this century. The most clever use of automobiles, however, was the brainstorm of Frank Archer, a Moxie executive.

You may recall from your history books that when motorcars were first driven on the streets in the 1900s, they frightened horses. Various experiments attempted to solve the problem. Uriah Smith of Battle Creek, Michigan, placed a stuffed horse's head on the front of a car, thinking it might calm down real horses. Carrying out Smith's idea, the Haynes-Apperson automobile company of Kokomo, Indiana, produced cars with horse's heads built on. However, Uriah's trick didn't fool the real horses, and the car came to be called "Apperson's Folly."

Moxie's Frank Archer saw potential for an advertising gimmick. He had an entire dummy horse mounted on an automobile chassis, rigged so the driver could sit in the saddle and steer. Eventually several of these "Moxiemobiles" toured the country, stopping at small and large towns and at state and county fairs, drawing crowds wherever they went.

A Moxiemobile

The drivers of these cars were called "Moxie Men," and they became a kind of celebrity. Although a number of Moxie Men might be touring the country at one time, Moxie ads nationwide featured a particular handsome, dark-haired fellow. It is said that some girls even fell in love with the Moxie Man in the ads, who was actually no more than the creation of an artist's brush.

The Moxie Man

Because of its advertising gimmicks—which included a Moxie Song and magazine ads along with Moxiemobiles and the Moxie Man—Moxie became so well known that in one year, 1920, it actually outsold the traditional number-one soft drink, Coca-Cola.

Celebrity Endorsements

It seems as if Americans will buy almost any product if a celebrity is willing to say he or she uses it. For generations, movie stars, singers, and sports heroes have added to their income by agreeing to pose for pictures with a manufacturer's product or by saying a few words in public about how good it is. Celebrity endorsements have long been a part of the soft-drink business.

As part of its advertising campaigns of sixty years ago, Moxie showed a drawing of Ed Wynn, a comedy actor, saying, "I may be a perfect fool, but I'm very particular." In his hand was a glass of Moxie. George

M. Cohan, a composer of many Broadway hits, including "I'm a Yankee Doodle Dandy," was featured on other Moxie ads.

Royal Crown Cola has used testimonials from '40s movie stars Bing Crosby and Hedy Lamarr. One of Pepsi's most famous stars in the '50s

Y. A. Tittle advertises Yoo-Hoo
Y. A. Tittle was a popular quarterback for the New York Giants in the 1960s. Just as Yoo-Hoo Chocolate Beverages had received endorsements from New York baseball players, it hired Tittle to sing its praises as well.

was Joan Crawford. As you've read, a number of New York Yankees endorsed Yoo-Hoo Chocolate Beverage in the '50s and '60s. In the '70s and '80s 7-Up has drawn on such athletes as Larry Byrd of the Boston Celtics, Magic Johnson of the Los Angeles Lakers, and Tony Dorsett of the Dallas Cowboys to praise its soft drink. Joan Rivers has told TV audiences that she loves the flavor of Diet Faygo, and Tim Conway has explained that Like is the only cola he would ever drink. Over the years Coke has used many celebrities in its ads, including Bill Cosby, Paul Anka, and Julius Erving.

---

* IDEAS & EXPERIMENTS 13 *

The "star system" of celebrity endorsements is a time-honored method for selling. You might investigate how well it works. Make note of the stars who appear on TV endorsing products—not just soda, but shampoo, hair coloring, fitness spas, batteries, etc. Then create a matching items quiz. On a sheet of paper, list the names of the stars in one column, and the products they endorse, in scrambled order, in another. How many of your friends can match the star with the product? What does this tell you about the effectiveness of celebrity endorsements?

In another test, ask your friends to name the products that are associated with certain stars. How often do your friends link a celebrity to a given product?

One of the most famous (and most expensive) uses of this star system was made by Pepsi-Cola, which, in 1984, paid singer Michael Jackson over seven million dollars to create a series of TV commercials. One ad simply showed Michael leaving his dressing room, going on stage, and singing one of his hit songs with a new set of lyrics about

Pepsi. The commercial received an amazing amount of attention; first, because Michael Jackson was the hottest superstar in rock 'n roll at the

A celebrity advertises Coca-Cola

time, and, second, because during the filming, some fireworks that were part of the set exploded and burned Jackson's hair. Not only were the fans worried about their hero, they were especially eager to see the commercial. Advance publicity was so great that newspapers published schedules of when it would be shown, just as if it were a regular television program. Pepsi also received extraordinary publicity with endorsements from singer Lionel Ritchie and former vice-presidential candidate, Geraldine Ferarro.

Slogans and Jingles

Another way soda poppers make their drink memorable is through catchy slogans, jingles, and songs.

Coca-Cola has the longest tradition of slogans, going all the way back to its inventor, John Pemberton, who declared in 1886 that Coca-Cola was "Delicious and Refreshing." Around 1900 Coke was said to be "Good to the Last Drop"; that slogan was discontinued, and, as you may know, it is used today by Maxwell House Coffee.

In 1909 Coke's advertisers said it "Has Character" and could be found "Wherever You Go." About 1915 ads advised, "Pause in the Mad Rush" and "Seek a Soda Fountain," where Coke would provide "Wholesome Refreshment."

"Thirst Knows No Season," said the Coca-Cola people in 1922, and in 1925 they stressed their number-one sales record by boasting, "It Had to be Good to Get Where It Is." Coca-Cola's national distribution allowed the company to brag in 1927 that Coke was "Around the Corner from Everywhere." In 1936 drinking Coke was "The Refreshing Thing to Do"; in 1957 it had become a "Sign of Good Taste." That word "refreshing," first used by John Pemberton, keeps coming up time and again in Coke ads, including 1959, when one could drink a Coke to "Be Really Refreshed."

Almost from the beginning, Coca-Cola had a nickname, the one we use today: Coke. You might think that the Coca-Cola Company would have liked that, since nicknames often indicate a kind of affection. However, at first Coca-Cola resisted. Some of its imitators had made use of that pet name—in particular, the Koke Company of Atlanta. Further, "coke" is also the nickname for the illegal drug, cocaine. Thus for years the Coca-Cola people wanted customers to "Ask for it by Full Name—Nicknames Encourage Substitution."

In the 1960s and '70s, Coca-Cola gave in to popular usage and began using the nickname in its slogans. "Things Go Better with Coke," said one series of ads; "Have a Coke and a Smile," said another; "Coke Adds Life," claimed a third. Most recently, Coca-Cola has again stressed its position as number one by saying, "Coke Is IT!"

Often soda-pop slogans are put to music. The "Coke Is IT" phrase can be heard in a variety of musical motifs, including pop (meaning popular music, not soda pop), country and western, contemporary crossover, marching band, samba, tropicale, and salsa.

7-Up has tried its share of slogans and songs, too. It has come a long way from advertising itself "For Home and Hospital Use" and as "A Cure for Seven Hangovers." Nowadays, 7-Up advertises itself as "The Un-Cola" in contrast to caffeinated drinks. In the 1970s it spent a lavish $40 million just to introduce a new advertising program with the slogan, song, and dance, "America's Turning Seven-Up."

Pepsi-Cola uses songs and slogans, too, but the company has also tried another gimmick. In 1938, its skywriter plane spelled out DRINK PEPSI-COLA eight times over metropolitan New York. Now its skywriters—yes, they're still active—simply write PEPSI in letters that cover ten miles of sky and can be seen for twenty miles in any direction.

"Be Sociable," said Pepsi in 1957 to counter Coke's "Sign of Good Taste" campaign. "Reduced in Calories" was the catch phrase when Pepsi lowered its sugar content in the late 1950s. Like 7-Up, Pepsi has stressed youth in its slogans: "Feelin' Free" and "Comin' Alive" were two phrases of the 1970s, and Pepsi scored an advertising triumph with a series of ads about "The Pepsi Generation." Soon people all over the country were using that expression to describe young folks—especially people under thirty years of age. Pepsi has worried about its "youth" image, and as recently as 1984 it would no longer compete for exclusive rights to sell Pepsi at Detroit Tiger games because the average baseball fan was too old for the advertising image Pepsi was trying to present.

The most famous jingle in all of soda poppery belongs to Pepsi, and it came about because of hard times. As you probably know, in the 1930s, the United States suffered a depression: the economy collapsed, and millions of people were thrown out of work. It was difficult for most people to make ends meet, let alone buy "luxury" items like soft drinks (even when a standard six and one-half-ounce bottle sold for a nickel).

Pepsi was near bankruptcy in the early 1930s. As a way of boosting

---

* IDEAS & EXPERIMENTS 14 *

From memory, make a list of all the slogans, jingles, and songs that you know from current soft-drink ads. What slogans are presently being used by:

Pepsi   Hires   7-Up
Royal Crown   Coke
Your Favorite Brand?

Can you hum or whistle the music that goes with the commercials? Can you recite the words? Which companies seem to you to have the most memorable slogans and songs? Analyze your memory patterns: Is there any relationship between the songs and slogans you remember and your favorite brands? Do you buy soda pop because of the slogans or songs a brand uses?

---

sales, its management hit on an idea: give the customer twice as much for the money. Pepsi broke with tradition by developing a new twelve-ounce bottle, which sold at the traditional five-cent price.

To launch an advertising campaign for the new size, Pepsi hired Alan Bradley Kent and Austen Herbert Croom to write a jingle. They were paid $2,500, a fair amount in hard times, but a pittance compared to what such work would pay today. They took the music of an old English hunting song, "D'ye Know John Peel," and wrote some new lyrics:

> Pepsi-Cola hits the spot.
> Twelve full ounces, that's a lot.
> Twice as much, for a nickel, too.
> Pepsi-Cola is the drink for you.

The tune was catchy, and so were the lyrics. *Life* magazine later declared that the Pepsi jingle was "immortal." Whether that jingle will live forever is debatable, but under this new advertising campaign, Pepsi rescued itself from going broke.

---

* IDEAS & EXPERIMENTS 15 *

Test the immortality of the Pepsi jingle. Can you find people who can hum the tune or recite the lyrics? Discreetly ask or silently guess how old these people are. Do members of "The Pepsi Generation"—people your age and a bit older—know the jingle?

Problems and Perplexities

Life in the soda-pop business has not always been a joyful carnival with singing and dancing. Many soft-drink companies that thrived years ago have died, and even Pepsi-Cola, one of the industry giants, has seemed to be on its deathbed more than once. Along with the amazing successes of the soft-drink industry in America, there have been problems and perplexities.

Pure Food and Drugs. In the early years of this century, consumers became concerned over the possible harmful effects of chemical additives in food and beverages. There was worry that packers of food were being outright dishonest about selling. Harvey Wiley, the author of a 1919 book on *Beverages and Their Adulteration,* reported this evidence of fraud:

> Once at a summer resort I saw a booth where orangeade was being sold. The beverage was presumably made while you waited. A few oranges were constantly rolling up an inclined plane and dropping into a machine and disappearing, and the juice was going out of a side exit. The food authorities, having examined this machine, found that the oranges were doing an endless stunt. . . . They escaped destruction altogether, while the reputed juice was wholly of artificial character.

In short, the oranges were for display only, and customers were being served a fake "orange" drink.

There were horror stories about what was going into soda-pop bottles and about the conditions under which pop was being bottled. People claimed to have found mice and beetles inside pop bottles. Others went to court claiming that whatever had been bottled in their soft drink made them sick. There were even cases where consumers played on the national interest in pure beverages by perpetrating a fraud of their own: in one instance, a man actually put poison into a soft-drink bottle, resealed the cap, then took the bottler and bottle to court. (The judge detected that the man's case was a fraud.)

Harvey Wiley, who had done considerable research on all sorts of foods for the U.S. government, went to work for *Good Housekeeping* magazine, where he wrote a monthly column in the 1910s warning homemakers of the possible dangers in foods and drugs. Of soft drinks, he wrote:

> The true soft drink is one which is palatable, cooling, and innocuous. It contains no drug or concoction which is in any sense intoxicating or habit forming. It is composed essentially of water, preferably carbonated with pure carbon dioxide, together with a syrup made of sugar and flavored with a fruit or harmless essence.

The U.S. government doubted that many soft drinks were pure and harmless. What were the ingredients in a bottle of pop? Could these be shown to cure diseases the way soft-drink makers claimed? Were carbonated beverages being bottled under sanitary conditions?

In 1906 Congress passed a Pure Food and Drug Act, which said, in essence, that products must be clean and pure, that they must contain

---

* IDEAS & EXPERIMENTS 16 *

For years, The Coca-Cola Company has fought the rumor that "Coke" stands for "coke" or "cocaine," and that there is cocaine in Coca-Cola. You know the fact: the slightest bit of cocaine is removed from Coke. Even before 1906, the amount of cocaine in Coke was so slight that one would have had to drink gallons in order to get even a small narcotic effect.

As an experiment, ask other people your age if they've heard the rumors about cocaine and Coke. How widespread is this myth today?

---

what is stated as their contents, and that they must actually achieve any medical or health-giving claims. "The average American," Harvey Wiley wrote at the time, "is daily taking a greater and deeper interest in what he eats or drinks."

The soft-drink companies quickly changed their advertising campaigns and moved to clean up their bottling acts. Moxie was no longer advertised as "nerve food," and other soft drinks dropped their health claims. Part of the Pure Food and Drug Act required products to be labeled as to contents, and at this point the Coca-Cola Company began to process coca leaves to remove the trace of cocaine found in them.

Alcoholic Beverages and Prohibition. Soda poppers were generally on the right side of the law when, in 1919, Congress passed the eighteenth amendment to the constitution. Under pressure from many citizen groups, legislators decreed that the manufacture and sale of alcoholic beverages were prohibited, thus leading to the name of an historical era in U.S. history: *Prohibition.*

Harvey Wiley, the pure-food watchdog, was strongly in favor of Prohibition, if only because it would keep children away from alcohol:

> I think the great majority of the parents in this country would prefer to see their children patronizing the soda fountain rather than the saloon, and if a choice between the two must be made, the soda fountain must certainly be preferred.

The very name "soft" implies that soda poppers had long seen their drink as an alternative to alcohol. Harvey Wiley argued that home-brewed soft drinks, such as those made with Hires extract, should be declared illegal because the fermenting process created traces of alcohol, though hardly enough to intoxicate a baby. On the other hand, Wiley argued that pure soft drinks might help people reduce their dependency on alcohol:

There is undoubtedly in man a tendency to drink other things besides water and milk, and if this tendency and drive can be controlled and directed into the consumption of harmless beverages containing no habit forming drug, it may aid greatly in the cause of temperance and in the restriction of the alcoholic habit.

Wiley foresaw booming sales of soft drinks during Prohibition. Some manufacturers tried to take advantage of this temperance movement in their advertising. Moxie, for example, capitalized on its strong taste (but nonalcoholic content) by suggesting that people could get some of the stimulation of booze without consuming any alcohol itself. Coca-Cola brought out a new slogan advertising itself as "The Drink That Cheers But Does Not Inebriate."

However, the predicted rise in soft-drink consumption never materialized. Adult Americans proved to be more interested in defeating the rules and regulations of Prohibition than in consuming soft drinks. You've probably heard about "rum runners" who brought illegal alcohol into the United States, using high-powered boats to evade federal agents. You may also know of "bathtub gin," the product of Americans who used their skill at home brewing to create illegal alcoholic drinks.

There are numerous stories about how people tried to sneak alcohol into the United States from Canada, where its sale was permitted. For instance, there's the tale of the elderly woman who hollowed out eggshells and filled them with liquor. (She was caught when an alcoholic egg burst in a customs inspector's hand.) Or the story about the men who dressed like priests and loaded their car with hootch, figuring the officer would not inspect the car of religious men. (Their figuring was wrong, and they went to jail.)

In pharmacies, people began looking for medicines that contained alcohol. Ironically, because of the Pure Food and Drug Act, the alcoholic content was printed right on the label. People thus bought and drank medicines in order to satisfy their craving for liquor. Recognizing this urge, some manufacturers raised the alcohol content in their elixirs, and in some cases what was advertised as medicine was actually plain wine.

Many people died during Prohibition when they drank things like hair tonic for their alcohol. Many hair tonics, rubs, and other potions contain "methyl" or "wood" alcohol that is poisonous. "Moonshine" whiskey—prepared in illegal backwoods stills by the light (and dark) of the moon—was often brewed improperly and led to deaths by alcohol poisoning.

The battle between pro- and anti-Prohibitionists was fierce. One famous anti-alcohol group, the Women's Christian Temperance Union, even launched an attack on *soft* drinks as potentially addictive and habit-forming. This, in turn, led William Allen White, editor of a newspaper in Emporia, Kansas, to write a satire in which he feigned worry about "men returning home sodden with Coca-Cola," men caught "in the grip of the Coca-Cola habit."

All in all, Prohibition probably neither hurt nor helped soda pop. There was no great boom in soft-drink sales, and when Prohibition was repealed in 1933, there was no great drop in soft-drink consumption.

The World Wars. Both World War I (1914–18) and World War II (1939–45) caused enormous problems for soft-drink makers. Sugar is the second largest ingredient in soda (water is first), and in war time, sugar is needed by the troops. Sugar prices soar and supplies are limited.

In 1916, for the first time since it was invented by John Pemberton, Coca-Cola sales decreased. The company simply couldn't make as much as it could sell because of the sugar shortage. Coke refused to reduce the amount of sugar in its drink or to use other kinds of sweeteners. In its advertising, Coke stressed its sacrifices with yet another slogan, "Making a Soldier of Sugar."

The government rationed sugar supplies and the soft-drink companies struggled. The Chero-Cola Company (which later became Royal Crown) established its own refinery to make sugar in Cuba, arguing that this imported sweetener could not be counted as part of its ration. Chero-Cola also bought huge quantities of Cuban sugar at a premium price, then nearly went bankrupt when the price of sugar dropped.

Pepsi-Cola actually did go bankrupt in the 1920s when it was stuck with stockpiles of overpriced foreign sugar. In fact, it was the sugar crisis of World War I that indirectly led Caleb Bradham, the inventor of Pepsi, to sell the company. After all his work making and promoting Pepsi for forty years, he was left owning nothing more than the drugstores where he had first sold his drink.

When World War II seemed imminent in the late 1930s, the soft-drink companies again stockpiled sugar in anticipation of a rationing system. However, the rationing board ruled that they could not use those supplies and forced them to sell sugar back to the government. Pepsi, for example, had to resell some 40,000 tons of stockpiled sugar.

Pepsi tried another strategy to solve the sugar shortage. It purchased sugar in Mexico, then had it turned into a sweet syrup called El Masco. For a period, the rationing board allowed Pepsi to import this syrup, accepting Pepsi's argument that syrup was not subject to the quotas. Then minds changed and El Masco was prohibited. Undaunted, Pepsi reacted by purchasing a sugar plantation in Cuba. It grew its own cane and produced its own sugar, just as Chero-Cola had done in World War I. Once again the government cried "foul" and passed a ruling that Pepsi's Cuban sugar must be *sold* in Cuba, not brought into the United States.

The Dr Pepper Company tried a different approach. Instead of trying to beat the quotas, Dr Pepper showed that soft drinks were important to the war effort back home.

Like most soft-drink makers, Dr Pepper had given up its claims to being a medicine or health food. However, in the 1940s, a Dr. Walter

Eddy conducted research that showed sugar and fruit acids give people an energy lift. Dr Pepper published Eddy's booklet, *The Liquid Bite,* explaining that drinking a Dr Pepper several times a day would help people work more effectively. The company adopted a slogan, "Drink a Bite to Eat," suggesting that workers preparing war materiel would improve their production if they took soda-pop breaks. Thus Dr Pepper could be seen as a kind of "patriotic" soft drink.

At this time, Dr Pepper adopted a new logotype showing the hands of a clock pointing to ten, two, and four, the hours at which Dr. Eddy advised people to take a soft-drink break. That logo was used by Dr Pepper long after the war ended, and today the company newsletter is called *The Clock Dial.*

For its part, Coca-Cola dusted off its "Making a Soldier of Sugar" slogan from World War I and introduced a new slogan, which, like Dr Pepper's, emphasized "The Importance of Rest-Pause in Maximum War Effort." Coke ads featured military people enjoying a Coca-Cola.

Coca-Cola's president, Robert Woodruff, also hit on a clever and patriotic plan by declaring that Coke was an American tradition and

Dr Pepper wartime ad

Coca-Cola wartime ad

that he wanted "to see that every man in uniform gets a bottle of Coca-Cola for 5¢ wherever he is and whatever it costs the Company." Woodruff began shipping entire bottling plants to war zones in Europe, Africa, and the Pacific. A total of sixty-four bottling plants were sent overseas, along with Coca-Cola managers and engineers. When General Dwight D. Eisenhower landed in North Africa in June of 1943, one of the first things he did was request machinery and bottling plants to produce six million bottles of Coke a month for his men.

Robert Woodruff and Coke were unquestionably generous in establishing these bottling plants, but their generosity didn't hurt the company one bit. It is estimated that over 95 percent of the soft drinks consumed overseas during the war were Cokes, and the American Legion, polling five thousand veterans of World War II, discovered that over two-thirds favored Coca-Cola as a soft drink. Coke had made itself a favorite brand of millions of military men.

After the war ended, the overseas bottling plants were *not* returned to American soil. They remained in foreign lands, pumping out Coke by the millions of gallons, not for American servicemen, but for the people of those countries. Coke now became the international soft-drink leader.

Today Coca-Cola is sold in over 150 countries and often outsells drinks native to those lands. It is so well known that "Coke" and "Coca-Cola" are said to be the first English words spoken by many foreign people. Coke's international growth was so great in the post-war years that in 1979 it was able to launch an advertising campaign showing young people of many different races and nationalities joining hands and singing, "I'd like to buy the world a Coke." The all-American soft drink had conquered the world in a way no army ever could.

Chapter 4

The Soft-Drink Wars

Competition among the soft-drink manufacturers has always been intense. Companies have swiped or "borrowed" ideas from one another, and they have freely imitated each others' flavors, bottle shapes, slogans, and even names. They have fought one another over sugar supplies and taken each other to court to protect their names, formulae, and trademarks.

Following World War II, that competition became even more spirited. In 1945 millions of veterans returned home and began raising families. Babies and soft-drink sales boomed, and the soda-pop companies strengthened their efforts to capture the mouths and hearts of a whole new generation of soft-drink consumers. An era of Soft-Drink Wars began.

The Pepsi Challenge

Perhaps the best example of the fierce competition was "The Pepsi Challenge" of the 1970s. Pepsi has always been second in cola sales to Coke. During the 1950s and '60s, Pepsi was able to reduce the size of Coke's lead through vigorous advertising, modern packaging, and

83

efforts to create a lower calorie beverage. The Coca-Cola Company was generally conservative, more cautious than Pepsi in trying out new ideas; after all, when you're number one you don't have to think as much about change.

In the '70s, Pepsi fired a loud shot in the soft-drink wars with a series of commercials in which people were shown taste-testing Coke and Pepsi, with Pepsi coming out on top. Pepsi-Cola had some research to back up its ads. Marketing Research, Inc. had conducted a national taste test with sampling that represented fifty million households. (This doesn't mean that fifty million people took the Pepsi Challenge; the survey was conducted with a *sample*—a smaller number of people— that was typical of families in fourteen "geographically dispersed" cities.) The testers bought Coke and Pepsi over the counter at grocery stores, ensuring that what people drank was the same beverage that the man, woman, or child on the street could buy. The soft drinks were chilled to precisely 42°F, a temperature some soft drinkers say is the best. The testers then went to the selected households and had people take The Challenge:

> [The] Product was brought into the house in opaque insulated bags and placed behind a screen measuring 18 × 24 inches.
>
> After being poured into clear plastic glasses behind the screen, one of the products was placed at the respondent's right hand and the other was placed at the respondent's left hand. Product was referred to as "the cola in your right hand . . . or left hand."
>
> The interview form indicated which hand would be used for the respective products so that no particular brand would always be either "left" or "right." Further, Pepsi-Cola was tested first in one-half the cases, while Coca-Cola was tested first in one-half of the cases.
>
> Before tasting each product, respondents were asked to sip water

to clear their palate. Ice was not used in the already chilled product so that it would not be diluted to any degree whatever.

After testing both products, respondents were asked the following question:

"NOW THINKING ABOUT THE TWO COLAS—ALL THINGS CONSIDERED, WHICH OF THE TWO DID YOU·LIKE BETTER, THE ONE IN YOUR RIGHT HAND OR THE ONE IN YOUR LEFT?"

In this study, Pepsi won its own challenge. 51.7 percent of those interviewed selected Pepsi, while 41.7 percent chose Coke and 6.6 percent had no preference. Regular Coke drinkers chose Pepsi 49.8 percent of the time and chose Coke only 44.2 percent. Regular Pepsi drinkers selected their own drink over Coke by a 58.2 percent to 37.3 percent margin. Marketing Research, Inc. summarized the results this way:

—Nationwide, more people prefer the taste of Pepsi-Cola to Coca-Cola;

—Nationwide, more Coca-Cola drinkers prefer the taste of Pepsi-Cola to Coca-Cola;

—Nationwide, more Pepsi-Cola drinkers prefer the taste of Pepsi-Cola to Coca-Cola.

You'll notice that Marketing Research, Inc.'s summary makes the victory sound more dramatic than it really was. (The company downplayed the fact that regular Pepsi drinkers chose Coke 37 percent of the time, almost four times out of ten.) Nevertheless, the data were clear enough that Pepsi launched an entire advertising program based on "The Challenge." In addition to TV, radio, and magazine ads, Pepsi had trucks touring the country (a bit like the Moxiemobiles of yesteryear), offering people a chance to take the Pepsi Challenge for themselves.

ANNCR: All across America People are taking the Pepsi Challenge. In Vermont, here's what they're saying.

KAREN RAIDT: Now that I tasted Pepsi, I'd rather buy that.

LOUIS TERREN: I'm not surprised when you sit side by side that people pick Pepsi.

CAMILLA PERCY: If you really want to be convinced yourself, try them side by side.

ANNCR: What will you say? Take the Pepsi Challenge and find out.

The Pepsi Challenge

These photos are from a storyboard prepared by Batten, Barton, Durstine & Osborne, Inc., a New York advertising agency, on behalf of Pepsi-Cola. They show the outline of a thirty-second TV commercial presenting the results of the Pepsi Challenge.

Naturally, Coca-Cola didn't accept the Pepsi Challenge without a fight. It hired comedian Bill Cosby to do a series of commercials. In one TV ad, he is shown in front of a simulated audience, doing one of his comedy routines. "Howcum," he asks the audience, "that in the Pepsi Challenge you never see *anybody* choosing Coke?" The audience laughs, and Cosby goes on to make fun of Pepsi, pointing out that despite the results of the Pepsi Challenge, more people still drink Coke than Pepsi.

In another commercial, Cosby stands before a huge photograph of former Pittsburgh Steeler, "Mean" Joe Greene. Cosby notes that in the Pepsi Challenge, taste-testers "sip" the two soft drinks. "Does this look like a man who sips?'' Cosby asks, pointing to Mean Joe. The clear implication is that Pepsi drinkers are sissified sippers, while Coke lovers chug down their soft drinks like tough guys. "Coke is the *real* thing," Cosby concludes.

Coca-Cola's president has said that in the long run,

> History will demonstrate that it [the Pepsi Challenge] was a big mistake for the competition [Pepsi-Cola], because it energized the biggest, strongest soft-drink distribution system in the U.S. and the world.

In other words, the Pepsi Challenge shook Coca-Cola out of its lethargy as number one. Indeed, when Coca-Cola changed its formula in 1985, some of its executives admitted that this was due to the success of the Pepsi Challenge. Americans really *did* feel Pepsi tasted better. In full-page advertisements in major newspapers, Pepsi gloated about the formula change. When Coke drinkers demanded and got a return to the old formula, Pepsi's spokesman, Ken Ross, exclaimed, "We now have the opportunity to compete with one product that lost to Pepsi in millions of taste tests and against one product the public hates." Ross was exaggerating public response, but for the immediate future, the gloves are off, and Pepsi and Coke will slug it out, bare-knuckled, over taste supremacy in the cola market.

Motivational Research and the War for Your Mind

The war among the soda poppers isn't always as open and obvious as it has been between Coke and Pepsi. Sometimes it is a subtle war, and rather than focusing on the merits of a particular soft drink, the manufacturers attempt to win you over in a different way.

In the late 1950s, advertisers became interested in the psychology of how people are persuaded to buy things. In a book called *The Hid-*

den Persuaders, Vance Packard told Americans about something called "motivational research," in which advertisers tried to dip into the subconscious mind of the consumer to find out what would *really* sell a product.

Now, the soda-pop industry always had some understanding of this technique. It knew, for example, that you can sell a lot of soda pop by having celebrities endorse it, because people subconsciously associate themselves with the star. Or you can sell pop by having a catchy tune that people hum and whistle without realizing it. Or you can sell soft drinks by showing a pretty girl in a bathing suit holding a soda because, subconsciously, men and women want to be with or look like her.

But in the 1960s and '70s motivational research and advertising became more intense and more expensive, and the soda companies risked vast sums of money on new psychological research. Among other things, they learned that Americans like to think of themselves as young, healthy, and vigorous. Increasingly soft-drink ads began to stress youth. Pepsi created new slogans: "Now It's Pepsi, for Those Who Think Young," "Come Alive, You're in the Pepsi Generation," and "Join the Pepsi People, Feelin' Free." Coke offered ads showing young folks engaged in vigorous work and play, drinking Coca-Cola. The Dr Pepper company launched its highly successful "Be a Pepper" theme, which featured youthful dancers who symbolized what being a Pepper was all about.

Perhaps the most elaborate youth campaign has been carried out by the Seven-Up Company. In the 1960s, 7-Up was described as "Wet and Wild," trying to get rid of its old image of a stomach remedy. In the 1970s, the company invested forty million dollars on the theme, "America's Turning 7-Up." Softball players, skateboarders, swimmers, horseback riders, and other youthful, athletic types were shown in vigorous pursuits. The theme was featured on television and radio commercials, on billboards and bus posters, and on grocery-store displays. Since the average cost of a bottle of pop in those days was about thirty-five cents, the Seven-Up Company thus spent the gross income from 120 million bottles of pop on advertising alone.

Does this sort of psychological advertising work?

The soft-drink companies are very secretive about the specific results of advertising campaigns and will seldom reveal precise statistics. However, here is one example that will help show the effectiveness of advertising:

In 1970 the Dr Pepper Company decided it wanted to make itself better known in New York City. It spent $1.3 million in advertising, including 13,200 bus posters, 6,600 subway ads, 150 television spot commercials, and 1,960 radio ads. The following year Dr Pepper sales in New York increased by 1.5 million cases (twenty-four cans or bottles per case). At the average price of thirty-five cents per can, Dr Pepper gained $9.1 million gross from this promotion, seven times the amount spent on the advertising.

In 1960 Americans were drinking an average of twelve gallons of soda per person per year; by 1982, that amount had more than tripled to thirty-nine gallons per year. Much credit for such increases must be given to the advertising and promotion people. It seems they have been successful in persuading Americans that the fountain of youth really is a soda fountain.

Be a Pepper

The Battle for International Sales

"Next to the electric outlet," *Time* magazine once observed, "hardly any American invention is as omni-present as ice-cold cola."

American soft drinks have gone worldwide in sales, led by Coca-Cola with some 1,500 bottling plants all over the globe. Coke sells an astonishing 35 percent of all the soda in the world. One out of every three soft drinks consumed any place on the surface of our planet is a Coke. The Coca-Cola Company has even been accused of "Coca Colonialization," of "invading" foreign countries and "capturing" their people and money by addicting them to the pause that refreshes.

Like Coke, Pepsi has also spread its sales worldwide. In 1906, Caleb Bradham registered the name "Pepsi-Cola" in Canada and began selling his soft drink; in 1907, he began bottling in Mexico. The Pepsi Company created *Compania Pepsi-Cola de Cuba* in 1935 and began selling in London, England, in 1936. Today Pepsi is available in about 150 countries, second only to Coke.

Often Coke and Pepsi skirmish over international sales. Once, in the Philippine Islands of the South Pacific, a rumor circulated that a Coke worker had fallen into a vat at the bottling plant and had dissolved in Coca-Cola. The rumor went on to say that rather than throw out that batch, the Coca-Cola people bottled it anyway, including the man's dissolved remains. The Coke people angrily denied the rumor (you could drown in a vat of Coke, but you wouldn't *dissolve*), and they suspected that it had been started by Pepsi people. Soon a new rumor swept the islands: yes, a worker had fallen into a vat of soft drink and dissolved, and, yes, he had been bottled, but this had happened in the Pepsi plant, not at Coke.

In Europe, Pepsi wages war with a fleet of trucks that invade cities where new bottling plants are opening. These trucks give out free samples of Pepsi, and they have been nicknamed "The Panzer Unit" after a German tank corps of World War II.

In Africa, Coca-Cola has hired tribal storytellers to tell about Coke as a way of introducing this unfamiliar beverage to the native people. When Pepsi-Cola opened a bottling plant in Africa, it invited the local church bishop to attend the ceremonies and offer his blessings, thus assuring people that the American drink was safe to consume.

In Hong Kong, China, Coke hired professional yo-yo champions to put on a display of their skill. In Brazil, Pepsi sponsored a parade with three marching samba bands.

Coca-Cola won the competition to be the first American soft drink bottled behind the communist Iron Curtain: a bottling plant was opened in Bulgaria on the shores of the Black Sea in 1965, with syrup and bottles imported from Italy and the carbonated water added by the Bulgarians. "Vsychko Vyrivi Po Dobre S Coke," said the Bulgarian advertisements: "Things Go Better with Coke."

Pepsi, however, won another important soda-pop battle behind the Iron Curtain: in 1958 it was chosen as the drink representing the United States at the Moscow World's Fair. The U.S. vice president,

Nikita Khrushchev drinks a Pepsi
Left center, Nikita Khrushchev; right center, Richard Nixon

Richard Nixon, offered the Russian premier, Nikita Khrushchev, a cup of Pepsi. After a sip, the premier said, in Russian, that this American soft drink was "a refreshing pause." Photographers from many nations snapped pictures of this scene, with the Pepsi logotype clearly displayed. The Coke people were irritated because Mr. Khrushchev had coincidentally used a phrase that is a variation of Coke's famous, "The Pause That Refreshes."

Pepsi and Coke are not *always* on opposite sides in the war for the international sales. In Japan they were accused of cooperating with one another in an attempt to drive Japanese soft-drink makers out of business. The two American companies had captured 52 percent of the Japanese market; combined, they were selling as much as all the Japanese bottlers. Much of this Pepsi/Coke supremacy was achieved through advertising, but the two were also accused of bribing restaurant owners not to serve Japanese soft drinks. Japanese bottlers responded by passing out leaflets saying Pepsi and Coke would melt one's teeth. There was violence at the city of Nara when a crowd of people, possibly Japanese bottling plant workers, slashed tires on Coca-Cola delivery trucks. A court case was settled when Pepsi and Coke agreed to pay $700,000 to help the Japanese bottlers become more competitive.

Pepsi and Coke are not the only U.S. companies fighting for the overseas market. Dr Pepper and Canada Dry, for example, are quite active, especially now that the two companies have merged. Canada Dry is sold in eighty countries through over 180 bottlers; Dr Pepper can be purchased in fourteen international markets. Both companies are active in the Middle East, Japan, and Latin America, as well as in the United Kingdom (Britain, Scotland, Wales, and Ireland). Canada Dry/Dr Pepper has also "reformulated" some of its beverages under the names of Mission and Salute for overseas sales.

There are some sales experts who feel that the domestic market in the United States is saturated with soft drinks, that Americans just won't be drinking that much more soda pop. Thus international sales are increasingly seen as a "growth area" for soft-drink manufacturers. It's safe to assume that as long as there are people on the face of the earth who haven't tried—or better, who don't regularly consume— American soft drinks, the U.S. soda poppers will be after them.

A Big Business Grows Bigger

There's an old saying in business, "Grow or die." It means that in a competitive, capitalistic economy, companies have to keep finding new markets for their products. If a business cannot expand its trade, it will wither away.

As huge as they may be, the major soft-drink companies—Royal Crown, Dr Pepper, Seven-Up, Pepsi, Coke, and others—have faced this problem of growth. There (probably) are limits to just how much soda pop people will consume, and limits to what advertisers can do to promote growth in the soft-drink industry. To protect themselves against a leveling off of business, several of the big companies have engaged in mergers with other companies and have diversified into other products.

In 1960, for example, Coca-Cola decided to get into a new business, and it merged with the Minute Maid orange juice company. Thus Coke was now an orange juicer as well as a soda popper. Coca-Cola has since branched out in other directions. Columbia Pictures, for instance, is a unit of The Coca-Cola Company. Columbia/Coke has produced such film hits as *Ghandi, Tootsie,* and *Ghostbusters,* and its television film division has made the series, *Hart to Hart, T. J. Hooker,* and *Fantasy Island.* Coca-Cola is in the wine business, having purchased Taylor Wines of California, and it even makes plastic wraps and picnic tableware through its Presto Products division in Appleton, Wisconsin. Within the Coca-Cola Company, Minute Maid has expanded its operations and now manufactures Hi-C Fruit Drinks, Maryland Club and Butter Nut coffees, and Ronco noodles and spaghetti. Coke/Minute Maid even sells Belmont Springs Water, putting it into the bottled-water business, from whence soft drinks originally sprang.

Pepsi-Cola has diversified as well. In 1965 it merged with Frito-Lay Company, makers of Frito Corn Chips, to become PepsiCo, Inc. This new company has bought into such businesses as sporting goods (Wilson), moving services (United Van Lines), and freight hauling (Lee-Way). PepsiCo rents cars and trucks, sells fork-lift trucks, and markets over one hundred different snack-food items. It has a wine division of its own and owns two fast-food chains: Taco Bell and Pizza Hut.

At one point in the 1960s, Pepsi even tried to get into the sugar business to support its soft-drink line. It created a sugar refinery in Montezuma, New York, but the business lost $8 million in its first two years and was sold to the Maine Sugar Company, which presumably knew how to make sugar profitably.

In diversifying, Pepsi and Coke have tried to protect themselves against fluctuations in the soft-drink market. If soft-drink sales stop growing, perhaps the moving business or the corn-chip trade will pick up. If people drink fewer carbonated beverages or if the government finds something harmful in diet soda and bans it, perhaps folks will drink fruit juice or wine or go out and play more tennis.

Other soft-drink manufacturers have used diversification and merger to create a wider array of products. The Canada Dry/Dr Pepper merger, for example, allowed the bottlers of each company to make and distribute a greater variety of soft drinks. Dr Pepper has also acquired the Big Red soft-drink company of San Antonio, Texas, and Welch's Grape Juice, making Dr Pepper, like Coke, a fruit-juicing soda popper.

Even the Moxie Company of New England has merged. In 1968 it bought NuGrape Company of Atlanta and merged with Monarch Citrus Products to create Moxie Industries, selling NuGrape, Kist, Suncrest, and Kickapoo Joy Juice soft drinks. (Kickapoo Joy Juice is named after a home-brewed concoction featured in the comic strip, L'il Abner. The soft drink made by Moxie Industries is much milder than its fictional counterpart, and may have inspired Mountain Dew and Mello Yello soft drinks.) Moxie's president, Frank Armstrong, said it took a lot of moxie (and money) to merge with the larger NuGrape Company. "It was like a guppy swallowing a whale," he admitted. The merger gave new life to Moxie, however.

Expanding the Soft-Drink Line

There's another way in which the soft-drink companies have worked to increase sales: by inventing new soft drinks and selling their line in many different packages.

Up through the 1950s, Coca-Cola was known as a "one-sight, one-sound, one-sell" company: it sold Coke in six and one-half-ounce green bottles, and all its slogans and jingles were dedicated to marketing that one product. Some Coca-Cola officials said confidently that the company would remain that way forever, that Coke was so strong it could survive indefinitely with one product offered in one size.

"Indefinitely" turned out to be a short time. In the 1950s, Pepsi challenged Coke's lead, in part because of its twelve-ounce bottle— "Twice as much for a nickel, too." Pepsi also brought out an eight-ounce bottle (to compete head on with Coke's six and one-half) and a thirty-two-ounce quart size.

Under pressure from its bottlers and dealers, Coke decided to experiment with ten-, twelve-, and twenty-six-ounce bottles. On January 27, 1955, these sizes were made available in a test-marketing project in Columbus, Ohio. The dam burst: the new Coke bottles were so popular they sold out almost instantly, and the store owners called for more. The field test was never completed, because the results were obvious. Coke had to change with the times.

If you'll look on grocery shelves, you'll see Coke available in a range of sizes up to three liters. Alas, the traditional six and one-half-ounce green bottle is gone; the only place you'll see it is in museums and antique stores.

Just as soft-drink manufacturers were experimenting with different sizes of bottles, the "tin" can was perfected as a way of selling soda pop. Prior to the 1950s, attempts to can soda were not successful. Because carbonated beverages contain mild acid, they eat away tin-can linings. Canned soft drinks had poor shelf life, and the bottle remained king.

In the 1950s, experiments with coated metals led to cans that wouldn't rot. Pepsi, R.C. Cola, and other soft-drink companies brought out the first cans, cone-shaped at the top, sealed with a traditional crown cap. The public liked cans: they were unbreakable, easier to store than bottles, disposable (in contrast to bottles, which carried a two-cent deposit), and could be chilled quickly in the refrigerator or on ice.

Soon, flat-top cans like the ones you buy today became available. At first these were opened with a punch, but soon a variety of "peel" or "pop-top" cans became available, cans you could open with your bare hands. Technology and materials changed further. Cans were made of lightweight aluminum rather than coated tin or steel, and they could be cast in a single piece rather than patched together from a "body" and two lids.

Bottle technology and materials changed as well. New plastics were discovered for lightweight, unbreakable bottles, though at first, like "tin" cans, plastic bottles dissolved on the shelf. Cheaper methods of glass molding led to the throw-away bottle—no deposit, no return. Bottle caps changed, and the old "crown cap" was replaced by aluminum twist-off and resealable caps.

All this is by way of saying that today you can buy soft drinks in just about any size and container you want. The Pepsi slogan, "Twice as much . . . ," has gone by the wayside, not only because the cost of pop has risen, but because so many bottle sizes exist. In fact, it's often difficult for consumers to figure out just how much they are paying for a soft drink. Prices range from inexpensive local or regional brands sold in large bottles to more expensive national brands that vary widely in cost, depending on whether you buy them in sixteen-ounce cans, large bottles, or by the cup at sporting events and movies.

Offering drinks in different sizes of containers may have contributed to the increase in soft-drink consumption during the 1960s, '70s, and '80s. In the late 1940s and early '50s, having a soft drink meant drinking six or, at most, twelve ounces. Nowadays, we routinely drink sixteen ounces at a pop.

However, another development in the soft-drink industry may have boosted sales even more: the soft-drink makers started inventing new brands, just as they had in the heydays of the 1880s and '90s.

* IDEAS & EXPERIMENTS 19 *

How much do you pay for soda? The mathematical formula for calculating cost is this:

$$\frac{\text{Cost of Container}}{\text{Size of Container}} = \text{Cost per Unit of Weight}$$

That formula will let you calculate pennies per ounce or dollars per gallon or whatever set of numbers you want to use.

For example, Coke originally sold for a nickel per six and one-half-ounce bottle, so:

$$\frac{5 \text{ cents}}{6\frac{1}{2} \text{ ounces}} = .76923 \text{ cents per ounce.}$$

Pepsi sold the twelve-ounce bottle for the same price:

$$\frac{5 \text{ cents}}{12 \text{ ounces}} = .41666 \text{ cents per ounce.}$$

At the present time, you probably pay about fifty cents for a sixteen-ounce can from a vending machine:

$$\frac{50 \text{ cents}}{16 \text{ ounces}} = 3.030303 \text{ cents per ounce.}$$

You're paying a lot more for your soft drinks than people did forty years ago.

Head off to the grocery store and do some comparison pricing. What are the best buys in soft drinks these days, both by brand names and by size of container?

In the 1960s Coca-Cola broke with its one-product tradition by introducing a fruit drink, Fanta. Soon after, it developed Sprite, a lemon-lime drink that looked and tasted a lot like 7-Up. Coke had moved into the un-cola market.

Vending machines may have had something to do with Coke's decision. Soft-drink machines usually dispense several different brands or flavors. It seemed to Coke that all the pop being dispensed from a single machine ought to be made by a single company. Thus whether people chose Coke, Fresca, or Fanta, they were spending their money on Coca-Cola products.

Pepsi-Cola figured this out, too, and even went into the vending-machine business as part of its diversification. Soon it was offering Pepi, Pepsi Light, Teem (a new drink that looked and tasted like 7-Up and Sprite), and Mountain Dew, a noncarbonated drink advertised with a rural "hillbilly" theme.

Coke developed a Santiba line of soft drinks, but those didn't sell well. Pepsi experimented more successfully with Patio soft drinks and mixers. Then Coke brought out Mello Yello, which was rather like Pepsi's Mountain Dew.

---

* IDEAS & EXPERIMENTS 20 *

Even with all the new brands on the market, the manufacturers are very protective about their old standby brands, especially Coca-Cola. Go to a fast-food restaurant that you know does *not* sell Coca-Cola. (Burger King is one; it only sells Pepsi.) Ask for "a coke." What does the clerk say? Then order a Pepsi in a Coke place (McDonald's, for example). What are the results?

In the early 1970s Coke saw the Dr Pepper Company invading some of its market, so Coke brought out a cherry-flavored drink that tasted like Dr Pepper and named it Mr. PiBB. Coke/Mr. PiBB put on an advertising blitz in New York City, and in one year its sales went from

Coca-Cola products

101   *The Soft-Drink Wars*

zero to 1.5 million cases, while Dr Pepper dropped from 1.5 million to 800,000.

The Pepsi/Coke battle went on. Coke went into the root-beer business with Ramblin'. Pepsi came back with On Tap root beer and topped Coke with an experimental apple soft drink called Aspen. There seems to be no end in sight to the new possibilities for soft drinks.

Perhaps as you begin experimenting with flavors in Part II of this book, you'll come across a subtle and engaging blend of flavors, plus a catchy name, that will make yours the soft-drink sensation of the next decade—or, at least, of your household.

Chapter 5

The Present and Future of Soft Drinks

You may have observed that none of the new soft drinks listed in the previous chapter was a "no-cal" or "diet" soda. So there's more to the story of new soda pops in the 1960s, '70s, and '80s. The "present" of soft drinks centers on attempts by manufacturers and the government to eliminate some of the less desirable or even harmful ingredients in the old-fashioned soda pop. We're in an era of soft-drinks as health foods.

For some time prior to 1960, soft-drink makers had searched for ways to cut down or eliminate the sugar in carbonated beverages. For one thing, sugar prices are not dependable; they go up and down with supply and demand, and in times of war, sugar is not only expensive, it may not even be available. For another thing, in earlier times sugared soft drinks were subject to spoilage, and it was reasoned that some sort of chemical alternative to sugar might have better shelf life in the store.

Most of all, however, soft-drink manufacturers sensed that the general public wanted sodas that contained less sugar. For instance, when

Pepsi-Cola reduced sugar content in the 1950s, its sales increased quite directly.

So what's wrong with sugar?

When it is taken in moderation, there isn't anything particularly harmful about it. Sugar is used by the body in the process of oxidizing or "burning" food, and it is a source of energy itself.

"Moderation" is the key word with sugar, and nutritionists are worried that the amount of sugar consumed by Americans is on the increase. More and more of it is used in our processed foods, and Americans have become more and more accustomed to using prepared and prepackaged foods at home, rather than making things from scratch. We also have a very powerful sweet tooth, and in addition to consuming sugar in everything from breakfast cereal to

---

* IDEAS & EXPERIMENTS 21 *

Read the labels on some packaged and canned goods you have around home. Remember that food labels list ingredients in the order of their composition percentage in the product. For example, a box of crisp rice shows milled rice as the first ingredient and sugar as number two. Thus there is already a considerable amount of sugar in the cereal before one adds milk and, in all probability, more sugar. (That same box has printed on it a recipe for ice cream pie, "chocolate spiders," and butterscotch bars, all of which contain high-calorie ingredients and are documentary evidence of the American sweet tooth.) Make a list of the hidden sources of sugar you consume through processed foods.

Note: Sugar can also appear in these foods under the names *corn syrup, glucose, fructose,* and *maltose.* Sometimes you'll see several of these ingredients used in a single processed food.

---

ketchup, we consume an extraordinary amount of sugar in snacks like candy bars. Then there is soda pop, which is roughly 50 percent sugar.

---

* IDEAS & EXPERIMENTS 22 *

The average soft drink contains about 125 calories. Essentially all of those calories come from sugar, which has about eighteen calories per teaspoon.

How many teaspoons of sugar are in an average soft drink? To figure the answer, divide as follows:

$$\frac{125 \text{ calories per drink}}{18 \text{ calories per tsp.}} = \text{teaspoons per drink}$$

Do the calculation. Then get some white sugar and a teaspoon, and measure out that number into a bowl. Look at the amount of sugar. Do you see now why soft drinks are a major source of sugar in many Americans' diets?

It is estimated that in the year 1821, the average American consumed ten pounds of sugar per year. One hundred fifty years later, in the 1970s, that figure had multiplied ten times, and the average American was consuming over one hundred pounds of sugar every year, about 4.4 ounces every day.

The most obvious effect of too much sugar in the diet is *fat,* and sweet things clearly contribute to people's being overweight. Researchers have also questioned whether sugar may contribute to tooth decay, heart disease, diabetes (sugar in the blood), kidney stones, urinary infection, arthritis (stiffness of joints), gout (swelling of joints), ulcers, and myopia (near-sightedness). In the early days of soft drinks, the manufacturers were fond of listing the diseases their herbal pops would supposedly cure. By rights, they probably should have listed the ailments that sweetwater can promote as well. If you compare the list above to those in Chapters 1 and 2, you'll see that in some cases sugar promotes the very diseases that root and herb soft drinks claimed they could cure.

Soft Drinks on a Diet

The search has been on, then, for a chemical sweetener that could substitute for sugar in soft drinks and other foods. One such sweetener was discovered as early as 1879 by a chemist, C. Fahlberg. He was not looking for a sweetener, but found one by accident. He had been working in his laboratory and, without washing his hands, put his fingers to his lips and tasted something sweet. The "something" turned out to be a chemical with the complex name of 2,3-dihydro-3-oxobenziososulfonazle. "Saccharin," as this compound is now called, is about five hundred times sweeter than sugar. At the end of the last century, many experiments were tried using it in food, including in soft drinks.

However, there were suspicions about possible harmful effects of saccharin. Harvey Wiley, *Good Housekeeping*'s watchdog, described it as a derivative of coal tar and said in 1919 that it "may be regarded as on the road to speedy exclusion." Many individual states banned its use, and in 1938 the Food and Drug Administration approved it cautiously, insisting that its use be clearly labeled on packages.

The biggest problem with saccharin, however, was not that people feared its side effects, but that it left a bitter aftertaste. Consumers simply wouldn't buy a saccharin-sweetened soft drink.

Lo-Cals and No-Cals. In the 1950s some progress was made toward getting rid of the aftertaste, usually by combining saccharin with other sweeteners. Kirsch's Beverages of Brooklyn, New York, and Cott's of New Haven, Connecticut, introduced "no-cal" sodas that sold some five million cases per year.

The real winner in the no-cal derby was a company named Royal Crown. R.C. had started out in 1905 as Chero-Cola, bottled in Columbus, Georgia, by Union Bottling Works. In one of the many lawsuits filed by Coca-Cola over the years, Chero-Cola was accused of trying to imitate Coke's name. Coke, in fact, was trying to establish that any drink using "cola" was infringing on Coca-Cola. The lawsuit dragged on for years until 1944, when Chero-Cola decided to change its name to Royal Crown. R.C. had modest, but not spectacular, sales over the years, but in 1959 they perfected the taste of a diet drink. R.C.'s scientists used a little bit of saccharin, but the major chemical sweetener was something called *cyclamate.*

Cyclamate had been discovered in 1937 by Michael Sveda, another scientist who forgot to wash his hands. Smoking a cigarette after working in his lab, Sveda noticed that it tasted sweet, and he tracked down a chemical, aspartylphenylanlanine, now known as cyclamate. It is some 150 times sweeter than sugar.

R.C. Cola brought out its new drink, Diet Rite, sweetened with cyclamate, and it took the country by storm. After only eighteen months on the market, it became the number four best-selling cola.

The soft-drink industry was astounded. Everybody knew that Americans were diet conscious. Everybody knew that a diet soft drink made a "perfect" diet food: it was sweet, tasted like a treat, but added no calories. Still, the success of this unknown cola surprised them, and the larger soft-drink companies rushed to get their own diet pop on the market.

Coca-Cola was reluctant to use its famous old name on a diet drink, so it brought out a new brand with a new name. A computer was programmed to create four-letter name combinations (marketing researchers said that four letters was just the right length for a soft-drink name). Among the thousands of combinations produced were FLUG, GAAG, and BURP. Coke rejected those, of course, and settled on TABB. Someone thought that two B's looked odd, so the name of the drink was shortened to TAB. (Ten years later, Coke liked the double B better and used it on Mr. PiBB.) TAB diet soft drink was a quick success and helped Coca-Cola regain some of the cola market it had lost to Diet Rite. Coke also experimented with expanding the TAB line to include other flavors: black cherry, ginger ale, root beer, lemon-lime, and strawberry. In the end, only the TAB cola sold well.

The Pepsi-Cola company was less reluctant to use its traditional name on a diet drink, and Diet Pepsi was introduced in 1964. Another low-cal Pepsi, Pepsi Light, was invented in 1967, but it did not use saccharin or cyclamate; it cut the amount of sugar in half and added lemon flavor to compensate for the loss of sweetness.

Banned in the United States. Suddenly, in 1969, the sweetness went out of the diet soft-drink business. Laboratory research on rats suggested that cyclamate was carcinogenic, or cancer producing. The research itself caused (and still causes) debate in soft drink circles. The rats were put on a diet of 5 percent cyclamate, roughly the equivalent of eleven pounds of sugar per day in the diet of an adult human. (Imagine eating that much sugar and what it would do to you.) In other words, the amount of cyclamate given the rats was extraordinarily high. As a Coca-Cola official observed, you'd have to drink about 550 soft drinks per day to get that much cyclamate into your system: "You'd drown before you'd get cancer." Nonetheless, the government countered, cancer is cancer, and cyclamate was banned.

Pepsi Light was hurt least by the ban, since it was a low-sugar drink and didn't use artificial sweeteners at all. Diet Rite suffered the most. R.C. claimed that the government's tests were "pseudo-scientific." The company even claimed that other soft-drink companies, jealous of Diet Rite's success, had financed the research, but nothing along those lines was ever proven.

The sugar industry was delighted with the cyclamate ban. They had fought diet colas right from the start, fearing they would lead to a decline in sugar sales. In one advertisement, the sugar companies printed a photograph of a healthy-looking, energetic boy. This young man, the ad said, just "delivered 82 morning papers, swam half a mile, hit a homer [and] needs a sugarless, powerless soft drink like a moose needs a hatrack."

R.C. had responded with an ad of its own: "Have you tried the soft drink that's got the 'Sugar Daddies' howling mad?" The sugar people retorted by attacking the notion that diet colas will slim one down. Soft drinks, they said, contain only about 2 percent of an average person's caloric intake. Cutting out soft drinks, they said, will never make fat people skinny.

It's probably correct that merely changing from sugared to diet pop will not reduce weight dramatically, but soft drinkers, not just the manufacturers, were upset with the cyclamate ban. When it was announced, there were "runs" on some stores, and people bought all the diet drinks they could, storing them for future use. It would seem that many Americans either didn't believe the rat research was valid or figured that they didn't drink enough diet soda to cause problems.

There turned out to be no need to hoard cyclamated diet drinks. Soda-industry chemists set to work quickly, and within months they had discovered a way to sweeten drinks with the old chemical, saccharin, masking its aftertaste with something called *glycine*. Ten months after the ban on cyclamate, diet soft drinks had recovered 65 percent of their sales.

The government had some reservations about saccharin, too, because it has also been linked with cancer in laboratory animals. The evidence against saccharin was not as strong as it was against cyclamate, and the government had to content itself with forcing the manufacturers to add a label: "Contains saccharin, a non-nutritive artificial sweetener which should be used only by persons who must restrict their intake of ordinary sweets." Later, the Food and Drug Administration strengthened this warning, making no bones about the dangers

Sugar-Free Hires advertisement

of saccharin: "Use of this product may be hazardous to your health. Contains saccharin, which has been determined to cause cancer in laboratory animals."

Despite the concerns and warnings, sales and consumption of diet soft drinks have continued to grow. Coca-Cola introduced Fresca, a diet lemon-lime drink that quickly captured a large share of the market. Hires brought out a diet root beer to compete with a raft of other diet root beers. In fact, virtually every name-brand soft drink is now available in a sugar-free form. Even Coca-Cola, which for years had refused to offer anything other than traditional sugared Coke, decided in 1982 that the time had come to bring out Diet Coke. Since Coca-Cola also makes TAB, you'll often see vending machines that sell both TAB and Diet Coke, putting Coca-Cola in competition with itself for your soda dollars. That helps you see how intense the soda-pop wars have become; the companies almost seem to be fighting with themselves.

The Nu Sweetener. In 1983, the diet soft-drink scene was made even more complicated by the announcement of a new kind of chemical sweetener. The G. D. Searle Company received approval from the Food and Drug Administration to sell a chemical called *aspartame* for use in a variety of sugarless foods. Searle sells this chemical under the brand name of NutraSweet.

As was the case with saccharin and cyclamate, aspartame/NutraSweet was discovered by accident. A scientist, searching for a medicine to help sufferers of ulcers, found a super-sweet chemical. Aspartame was tested on laboratory animals for over a decade before it was declared safe for use.

Aspartame is over 200 times sweeter than sugar, so a little of it goes a long way. However, it is also quite expensive, costing roughly ninety dollars per pound, in contrast to four dollars per pound for saccharin. To save money, the soft-drink companies first started using aspartame in a one-to-three mix with saccharin in their beverages.

In 1984, however, the makers of Squirt, a grapefruit soft drink, set a precedent by announcing that their Diet Squirt would be sweetened with 100 percent NutraSweet at no extra cost to the consumer. Squirt felt that people were worried enough over saccharin to go for a drink using aspartame alone. They proved to be right, and soon most manufacturers followed suit.

111   ***The Present and Future of Soft Drinks***

In changing, they also set off another skirmish in the ongoing war between Pepsi and Coke. Diet Pepsi changed over to 100 percent NutraSweet early in the game, and its TV commercials showed cans of Diet Pepsi and Diet Coke side by side, the Coke with a drooping straw because of its saccharin content. Soon after, Coke made the switch to pure NutraSweet and countered with an ad showing trucks lined up ready to ship the new Diet Coke to every store in the country.

In the midst of all this celebration of the value of NutraSweet/aspartame came some voices of concern. Consumer protection groups protested that the testing done on NutraSweet had been done too quickly and that, under pressure from food processors, the Food and Drug Administration had approved the drug prematurely. They cited a number of complaints about possible side effects from aspartame-sweetened products, including headaches, rashes, dizziness, and even seizures. The consumer groups questioned the reliability and accuracy of some of the tests that had been performed, and they argued that more research must be done, especially on what happens to aspartame after it decomposes, possibly into dangerous byproducts.

It would seem, then, that the nu sweetener may not be the perfect solution to the sweetening problem in diet soft drinks. One has to suppose that considerably more testing and research will take place, and it may turn out that NutraSweetened soft drinks may also have to carry a warning label.

So Where's the Caffeine?

When John Pemberton mixed up the very first batch of Coca-Cola syrup in 1886, he added a pinch of a bitter powder called caffeine, derived from the cola leaf. Caffeine is a chemical—methylaxine—found in a number of plants. Its most common source is coffee beans and tea leaves. In the early part of this century, in fact, much of the caffeine in colas actually came, not from cola leaves, but from tea sweepings—the tiny crumbs of tea that were left over after teabags were packaged. Caffeine gives people a "lift" by elevating the blood pressure and increasing heart rate. The effects of caffeine have always been a part of "the pause that refreshes" for Coke and other colas.

Concerns about the effects of caffeine have been recorded for years. As you've seen, some soda pops boasted of being caffeine-free in the early 1900s. About that time, Harvey Wiley, the *Good Housekeeping* pure foods expert, issued a warning to parents, "who refuse to allow their children to drink coffee or tea at home, on the assumption that it may prove injurious to them" while "unwittingly permitting them to drink the active principle of these two bodies, namely caffein, under the guise of coca cola, pepsi cola, tokola, cola coke, and other similar beverages."

Experts generally agree that taken in moderation—in amounts between fifty and two hundred milligrams per day—caffeine does not do measurable harm. A cup of coffee will ordinarily contain eighty to one hundred twenty-five milligrams per cup, a cup of tea forty to eighty milligrams, a twelve-ounce soft drink thirty to seventy milligrams. From those figures, you can see that a person having two cups of coffee or tea per day, or no more than two soft drinks, would be in the moderate consumption range. However, for a child, with a smaller body weight than an adult, two soft drinks might represent more than a "moderate" amount of caffeine.

Beyond two hundred milligrams per day, the effects of caffeine become measurable, though experts are quick to say that much more research is needed to determine precisely how it affects the system. Children who consume too much caffeine have been shown to become fidgety, nervous, and irritable. Adults who consume too much coffee can develop headaches and nausea. Preliminary research has shown that caffeine may be linked to breast disease in women and to under-development of the brain in children, leading to poor coordination. When caffeine was administered to female laboratory rats, their birth rates dropped and some of the babies were born deformed.

With this growing body of evidence, and with Americans' present concern over the harmful effects of food additives, it's not surprising that caffeine-free sodas have suddenly emerged.

In the 1970s, 7-Up had advertised itself as an "Un-Cola," an alternative to Coke. The company had even brought out soda-fountain glasses shaped like the famous Coke glass, but upside down. In the 1980s, 7-Up dusted off that advertising program and ran it again, this time emphasizing the caffeine-free nature of its drink: "Never had it. Never will." 7-Up sales soared.

Pepsi-Cola was the first company to enter this new market, developing a drink called Pepsi-Free, which quickly captured 50 percent of the caffeine-free market. Pepsi-Free is available in both sugar-sweetened and sugar-free versions. Coca-Cola eventually followed, introducing decaffeinated Coke, Diet Coke, and TAB. When you think about all the possibilities, the choices among these drinks now seems dizzying. You can buy regular Pepsi-Cola, Diet Pepsi, and Pepsi Light, plus regular Pepsi-Free and Diet Pepsi-Free. You can also choose regular Coke, Diet Coke, caffeine-free Coke, and caffeine-free Diet Coke, plus regular and decaffeinated TAB.

Choices, choices

As if all those choices were not enough, some soft-drink manufacturers have now discovered that Americans have become conscious about the amount of sodium in their diet and are advertising their drinks as low-sodium. One can imagine new versions of old favorite drinks, regular and sodium-free. You may need to take a computer to the store with you just to keep track of all the soft-drink combinations that are available.

---

* IDEAS & EXPERIMENTS 23 *

In this chapter, you have been given quite a bit of information that can prove worrisome to you. Soft drinks are not simple, pure, and harmless drinks; every soda pop—whether naturally or artificially sweetened—contains ingredients that, if consumed in excess, can potentially harm you.

It is difficult to calculate what "excess" means, though in soft drinks it generally means more than one or two per day.

What is your rate of consumption of soda pops? Do you grab one at lunchtime and then another after school and a third and fourth while watching TV? Do you drink more over the weekends? Just how many soft drinks do you consume during a week?

Keep track of your soft-drink habits for a week or more. Note every soda pop you consume, whether regular, diet, or decaffeinated. When you've finished, spend some time studying the numbers. Given what you've read here, you may want to change your soft-drink habits. Or you may discover that you are a moderate user of soft drinks and that your rate of consumption is acceptable. In either case, you'll have read the facts and collected information so that you can make an informed decison.

What Next?

So the quest for new markets continues, here and abroad. Soda-pop manufacturers are in fierce competition with one another, both to capture an increasing share of the existing market and to be the first kids on the block with a new flavor or new merchandising idea that will create even more business.

What does the future hold? It seems difficult to predict precisely where soft drinks will go in the future, but some trends seem clear.

Information collected by *U.S.A. Today* newspaper has shown that in the past twenty years, soft-drink consumption has steadily risen, from about ten gallons per person in 1960 to thirty-eight gallons in 1982. In that same period, average consumption of plain old water dropped from about seventy gallons in 1960 to approximately forty-two in 1982. In other words, Americans now drink just about as much water as pop. One implication of this information might be that sales of soft drinks will continue to rise while consumption of water will drop. However, a more reasonable speculation is that soft-drink and water consumption are likely to level off at about forty gallons each per year. In short, the fears of soft-drink manufacturers that the domestic market is saturated may come true shortly. That would probably mean even more intense competition here in the United States, plus redoubled efforts to find new consumers in other countries.

The same data also show a steady increase in the sales of diet pop from 1960 to 1982, and a decrease in the percentage of the market controlled by regular sugared soft drinks. It's interesting to note, however, that despite all the fuss over diet drinks, they still only command about 20 percent of the market. Four times out of five, people reach for a sugared drink. It seems safe to predict, then, that although the soft-drink wars over diet and caffeine- and sodium-free drinks may escalate, sugared soft drinks will continue to be popular.

Actually the word "sugared" may be inappropriate here, because in recent years a number of major soft-drink manufacturers have shifted away from using sugar in their sweetened drinks, substituting corn syrup, which has the advantage of being less expensive to make and use and less subject to wild price fluctuations. We can predict with some confidence that the manufacturers will continue to search for an inexpensive alternative to sugar in soda pop and that other kinds of sweeteners will be explored.

Further, we know that the struggle to find the perfect artificial sweetener is not over. NutraSweet may prove to be the winner of the sugarless derby of the 1980s, but what sorts of chemical sweeteners may appear in the near or distant future? We don't know what they'll be, but it seems reasonable to assume that new ones will be found.

Despite all the changes in the soft-drink field over the years, one aspect of the selling of soft drinks hasn't changed very much. John Pemberton of Coke, Caleb Bradham of Pepsi, Charles Hires of Hires, and many other soda poppers designed drinks they thought would cure people's ailments. Many of their claims were not true, and thanks to the Pure Food and Drug Act, soda poppers can no longer make outrageous promises. But if you look at modern advertising, especially the hidden and unstated appeals, you'd really think that soda pops were some sort of amazing health food. The ads seem to say that if you drink lots of pop, you'll be relaxed, popular, fit, and vigorous.

Suppose all those claims were really true or were to come true sometime in the future!

Speculate about the "perfect" soft drink of the future:

—It might be vitamin-enriched so that it not only tasted good but sustained some of your nutritional needs.

—It would probably be sugar-free, but possibly sweetened with a miracle ingredient that, instead of being harmful to laboratory rats, made them (and the people who drink pop) smarter than ever.

—It might come in a container that would dissolve after use so you'd no longer have empties to deal with.

—It might come in powdered or tablet form so you wouldn't have to lug heavy bottles home from the store.

The chances are, whatever we've thought about for the future is being considered in one way or another by someone in the soft-drink industry today. It is clearly part of the Great American Soft-Drink Tradition that soda poppers never stand still.

PART II

Making & Using Soft Drinks

Introduction to Part II

When I was a boy, my family regularly took a summer vacation in Maine. Over the years, we developed a number of friends among the "down Easters" who lived in the town of Weld, Maine, and a highlight of the summer was renewing acquaintances. Among our friends were a farmer and his wife who lived a few miles out of town.

One hot summer day when I was perhaps eight or ten years old, we visited the farm, and the farmer's wife served me a root beer.

"We make it ourselves," she explained.

I was astounded. I guess I had always supposed that root beer was just a factory product; the idea that you could make it at home fascinated me.

The farmer then told a story about home-brewed root beer. When *he'd* been a boy, his family had been seated at the dinner table on another hot summer day. They were distracted by a pounding on the dining room floor. They couldn't figure out the noise and even thought it might be ghosts. Finally, they searched the cellar and discovered that their home-brewed root beer was popping its corks in the heat. The corks, hitting the basement ceiling, were making the sound.

I think it was that down-East homemade root beer and the story of

121

those corks that set me on the road to becoming a soda popper. But it was many years before I brewed my first batch of pop. Oh, I'd *talked* about it. I'd told my wife the story about Maine, saying that someday I'd like to brew my own root beer. However, I never did anything about it. Soda poppery remained mostly a memory and a dream.

Then, for my birthday several years ago, my wife surprised me with a gift, consisting of:

One bottle of Hires' Root Beer Extract.
Instructions for home brewing.
A bottle capper.
A supply of bottle caps.

I was in business, and the very next day I brewed my first batch of root beer.

It was good stuff. Homemade root beer has a stronger flavor than store-bought, a yeasty taste. My family and I preferred it to the commercial root beer we'd enjoyed in the past.

After several batches, I became curious about other flavors of home-brewed pop. At the library, I found some old recipe books including instructions for making ginger ale at home. I tried that successfully, creating a ginger ale I much preferred to commercial pop.

Then I was off into other experiments, using orange juice, grapefruit juice, herbal tea, vanilla flavoring . . . anything I could think of that might make a good soft drink. In the process, I did more reading about the history of soft drinks, and somewhere along the line, in between brewing batches of soda pop and reading about it, the idea for this book emerged.

Here in Part II I'll share my experiences as a brewer of soft drinks and encourage you to become a practicing soda popper.

I will describe two techniques for making soft drinks at home. The first follows a time-honored method of adding yeast and sugar to water to create a drink that must be bottled. This method is simple enough, but it requires some special equipment. Read through the next section, *Brew and Bottle It Yourself.* If that technique seems too complicated, or if it involves more time than you have to spend, skip to the following section, *The Home Soda Fountain,* and read about ways of making pop by the glass using commercial club soda and flavorings.

Brew and Bottle It Yourself

The basic home-brewed soft-drink recipe works this way:

Yeast + Sugar + Water + Flavoring → Soda Pop

Yeast, which is actually a small plant, "feeds" on sugar and grows rapidly, producing as a byproduct, carbon dioxide, the fizzmaker in pop. Yeast is also used in the kitchen to make bread rise by the same process. In bread, the carbon dioxide is "trapped" inside the loaf, causing it to swell or rise. In soda pop, the carbon dioxide is trapped inside the bottle and thus "carbonates" the water.

NOTE: *This reaction of yeast and sugar is a process of fermentation and produces a small quantity of alcohol as a byproduct. Home-brewed pop contains less than 1 percent alcohol and is not intoxicating. Nevertheless, some people feel that fermented soda pop is not properly considered a soft drink. Before you brew any yourself, show this note to the adults with whom you live and get their permission to proceed. If you decide not to brew soda pop using this method, simply flip to the next section.*

Equipment: You'll need the following to make soft drinks at home:

Large pot or kettle
Candy thermometer
Clean, empty beverage bottles
Bottle capper
Bottle caps
Funnel
Ladle

For bottles, collect twelve-ounce empties that originally had "crown cap" lids, the kind you pry off with an opener, not the twist-off, resealable kind.

The bottle capper and bottle caps may be difficult to find. Look in the yellow or white pages of the phone book to find the name of a store that specializes in supplies for homemade wine and beer. It may be that you'll have to wait until you're in a larger town or city to find such a place, or you may find that an area hardware store or kitchen specialty shop stocks this equipment. The capper is simply a device that squeezes the cap around the neck of the bottle, creating a tight seal.

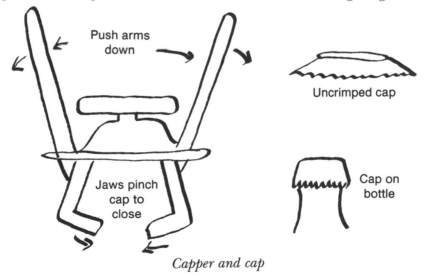

Push arms down

Uncrimped cap

Jaws pinch cap to close

Cap on bottle

Capper and cap

The Basic Recipe (makes 12 twelve-ounce bottles)

2 tablespoons extract or flavoring
1½ cups sugar or other sweetener
144 ounces water (12 bottles)
⅛ teaspoon dry active yeast

1. Heat the water in a large pot or kettle to about 125°F on your thermometer or to "lukewarm" to the touch.

2. Stir in the sugar and dissolve it. You may want to adjust this amount "to taste." I like to use less sugar, about 1¼ cups per batch. This creates a "drier" soda pop with about 33 percent fewer calories than commercial pop. You can also use other sweeteners than white sugar. As you create different flavors, experiment using brown sugar, molasses, honey, or corn syrup.

3. Stir in yeast and dissolve it.

4. Add the extract or flavoring. If you can find root beer extract, try that, but the Hires Company stopped making it in 1983 and you may have difficulty locating some. Other store-bought extracts that produce good soda pop are: vanilla (to make cream soda), lemon, orange, cherry, and banana. Adjust the amount of extract to taste. Resist the temptation to use a lot of extract—a little creates a great deal of flavor.

5. Bottle the pop by ladling it through a funnel into sterilized bottles. (To sterilize bottles, fill them half full with water, place them in a pan half filled with water, and boil gently for fifteen minutes. Then empty the bottles.)

6. Cap the bottles. Place a cap on top of the bottle, open the "wings" of the capper, place the capper on the cap, squeeze the wings to crimp the cap closed.

7. Place the bottles in a warm place, away from cold drafts and breezes, for three to five days. In winter, place the bottles near (but

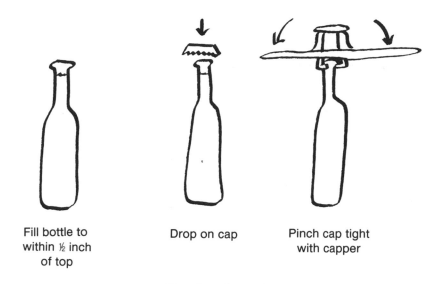

| Fill bottle to within ½ inch of top | Drop on cap | Pinch cap tight with capper |

Capping the bottle

not right next to) a radiator. In the summer, place them in any warm spot, but never in direct sunlight.

8. After three days, uncap one bottle and see how much it fizzes. If you want more carbonation, let it sit a day or two more.

9. Refrigerate the bottles. (Don't store them in the cellar the way my farmer friend in Maine did; although a basement may be cool enough to preserve your pop, the 'fridge works much better.)

You'll have to do a lot of experimenting to find a recipe that is exactly to your liking. Use your Soda Poppery notebook to keep precise records. For each batch record the ingredients as well as the length of time you store your bottles. I've found that even when I put my soft-drink bottles in the same place consistently, some batches seem to create more carbonation than others. The amount of yeast you put into the mixture will affect carbonation (cut down a bit on the yeast during the summertime), as will the precise temperature of your "lukewarm" water. Good record keeping will help you get consistent results.

127   Making and Using Soft Drinks

Finally, label your bottles of pop carefully, especially if you begin experimenting with a variety of flavors. You can get press-on labels at most grocery stores, and you might even do some fancy lettering on some labels.

Plain   Fancy

Soft-drink labels

Troubleshooting. The basic recipe is more or less foolproof, and people have been using variations of it for over two hundred years in this country. However, from time to time a batch may not turn out quite right. If you've kept careful records, you can probably figure out the problem yourself, but here are the three major ones:

1. *No fizz at all.* This probably means that your yeast didn't react. If you used water that is hotter than lukewarm, you may have killed the yeast; on the other hand, the water might have been too cold. Or, you may simply have had a bad batch of yeast. Buy another packet and start over.

2. *Too little fizz.* Either you didn't let the pop sit long enough, or you didn't keep it in a warm enough place. This can be cured without tossing the batch; just move the bottles to a warmer spot for a day or two and see what happens.

3. *Too much fizz.* I've opened some bottles that proved to be real gushers. (I always open the first bottle from each batch over the sink

just in case.) Either you've used too much yeast or kept the bottles in too warm a place or let the bottles stand too long before refrigerating.

• Root Beer from Roots

The Hires Company no longer makes root beer extract, which, in turn makes the brewing of homemade root beer more difficult. However, you can make root beer the *real* old-fashioned way, from roots.

By tradition, almost anything can go into root beer.

The cartoonist Al Capp once said of his famous comic-strip brew, Kickapoo Joy Juice, "You can just throw in anything handy . . . anything crawling by, maybe a dead horse to give it body." We presumably don't want to throw a horse or crawling things into root beer, but compare the lists of ingredients for these two recipes, the first from Edward Grieve's *Culinary Herbs and Condiments,* published in 1934, the second from Solveig Paulson Russell's *Peanuts, Popcorn, Ice Cream, Candy and Soda Pop,* written in 1971:

Grieve's Ingredients	Russell's Ingredients
Sorrell Leaves	Sassafras Root
Horehound Leaves	Spicewood Bark
Dandelion Roots	Wintergreen Leaves
Lemons	Cherry Bark
Red and Black Currants	Hops
Ginger	Coriander
Brown Sugar	Molasses
Water	Water

As you can see, the only thing they have in common is water. Russell's ingredients are closer to the kind of taste you expect from commercial root beer, chiefly because sassafras has always been the major flavor of root beer. However, even he suggests that other herbs in root beer could include sarsaparilla, pipsissewa, flag, spikenard, hemlock tips, licorice, dandelion, and dock.

If you want to brew your own authentic root beer, visit a health-food store where herbs and roots are sold. Check first for sassafras roots, second for sarsaparilla bark. Look also for cherry bark or dandelion roots. Find one or several of those, then steep about two ounces of roots in twelve ounces (one soda bottle) of boiling hot water for about thirty minutes. Strain the roots and herbs from the water and add it to 132 ounces of lukewarm water (eleven bottles) to give you 144 ounces of water. Then just follow the basic soft-drink recipe outlined at the beginning of this section.

• *Mock Root Beer*

If you can't find the right herbs at the health-food store, or if you just want a quicker recipe, you can make a good imitation root beer using Celestial Seasonings Emperor's Choice herbal teabags, available at most groceries and health-food stores. This contains a number of roots and herbs, including ginseng root. Soak four teabags in twenty-four ounces of hot, almost boiling, water for thirty minutes. Remove the teabags, add one teaspoon of vanilla extract, and a dash of powdered ginger. Add 120 ounces lukewarm water and follow the basic recipe, using dark molasses instead of sugar for the sweetener.

• *Ginger Ale*

Here's a recipe for homemade ginger ale that will turn you away from store-bought sweetwater. It produces an "authentic" ginger ale that is quite like English ginger beer in taste.

Buy a piece of fresh ginger at the grocery. This is a gnarled and twisted root that will cost about seventy-five cents for a chunk the size of your thumb. At home, cut the ginger into small slices and pound them gently with a hammer to "bruise" them and release the essence. Boil the ginger in twenty-four ounces of water for twenty minutes, then strain and add to 120 ounces of lukewarm water. Follow the basic recipe to its conclusion.

• Herbal Tea Pops

By now you've probably gotten the idea of how the basic recipe can be altered to accommodate many different kinds of fresh herbs. Herbal teas such as those made by Celestial Seasonings can be used to create some wonderful soft drinks, all of them caffeine-free. Try using some Red Zinger; this will produce an attractive red soft drink with lots of bite. Sleepytime will produce a minty soda pop. Almond Sunset makes, you guessed it, a pleasant almond soft drink. With any tea pop, begin by steeping four tea bags (or more, or fewer, to taste) in 24 ounces of almost boiling water to create a superstrong tea. Then add that to 120 ounces of lukewarm water to create 144 ounces and proceed following the basic recipe.

• Fruit Juice Soda

You can use fruit-juice concentrates to make a home-brewed soft drink. I like to start with grapefruit juice to create a soda that is, to my thinking, a lot tastier than commercial grapefruit pop. Or you can use orange juice to make something that will outmuscle store-bought orange. I haven't tried grape or apple juice, but you might want to give them a splash.

Begin by mixing a twelve-ounce can of concentrate with three cans of water—in other words, follow the instructions on the can. Then add the mixed juice to 96 ounces of hot water. Let the mixture cool until it is lukewarm, about 125°F, then proceed with the basic recipe. Orange, grape, and apple juice are quite sweet naturally, and you can cut down on the amount of sweetener to approximately one cup. Grapefruit juice is sour, and you may want to use as much as 1¾ cups of sweetener with it. Experiment.

Incidentally, you'll note that fruit pop contains much more water than just plain fruit juice. (You start with juice, then dilute it twofold.) Yet the pop still tastes good because of the effects of carbonation. The carbon dioxide in the pop adds zing and effervescence, so you can use less flavoring. Commercial soft drinks made from real fruit contain even less juice. That's another reason why, in my opinion, home-brewed soda pop is better than store-bought.

Other Ideas and Experiments. Just about any mixture containing flavoring, yeast, sugar, and water will create a carbonated drink. Explore other possibilities for flavoring ingredients, using the basic recipe as a guide. You can try experiments using:

- commercial flavorings and extracts
- fruit juices and syrups from canned fruit (peaches, pears, pineapple)
- fruit syrups from real fruit (the next section explains how to make these)
- commercial syrups (for example, blueberry pancake syrup)

Remember the spirit of Charles Hires, John Pemberton, Caleb Bradham, Augustin Thompson, and the other soda poppers of the last century. Drink a toast to their memories with your spectacular new drink.

The Home Soda Fountain

An easier way to make soft drinks at home is by the glass. Simply add three basic ingredients together:

Carbonated Water + Sweetener + Flavor → Soda Pop.

This time, you buy carbonated water or club soda at the grocery store. Buy the largest bottle of the cheapest brand you can. Although the manufacturers try to claim there are differences, one brand is just about the same as another.

Next you'll need to make a sugar syrup to serve as sweetener.

• *Sugar Syrup*
Add two cups of white or brown sugar to one cup of water and boil gently in a saucepan for five minutes. (*Be careful:* Hot sugar syrup can cause nasty burns.) Let the syrup cool and keep it in the refrigerator.

• *Soda Fountain Pop: Basic Recipe*

   1 glass carbonated water at room temperature
   1–2 teaspoons sugar syrup

133

Flavoring or extract to taste (the amount you add may vary from just a drop of some essences to a half teaspoon of weaker extracts)

For flavorings, use commercially prepared extracts and essences, which you'll find in the baking section of your local grocery store. If your store has a place where ingredients for homemade candy can be found, look there, too, for interesting flavors. In surveying available flavors, I've found the following for sale within just a few blocks of home:

Anise	Licorice
Apricot	Lime
Banana	Maple
Blackberry	Nutmeg
Black Walnut	Orange
Butter	Peppermint
Butter Rum	Pineapple
Butterscotch	Plum
Cherry	Raspberry
Chocolate	Sassafras
Cinnamon	Spearmint
Clove	Strawberry
Coconut	Vanilla
Grape	Walnut
Horehound	Watermelon
Lemon	Wintergreen

Not every one of these flavors would make a good soft drink (I've never tried to make watermelon soda pop and never will), but you can see the possibilities, using these either alone or in combination.

With just a few flavors in hand, you're now ready to set up a home soda fountain similar in spirit to those of the 1890s. Look back to Chapter 1 of this book and study the flavors that were tried. Make some exciting combinations yourself and name them. Discover which flavors are your family favorites.

• Walnut Cream

In Chapter 1 I said I'd tell you how to make this kind of soda. It's simple: just use walnut flavoring and vanilla in equal amounts. Try a half teaspoon of each for starters and then adjust the recipe to taste.

A Word on Colorings. Many soft drinks made from flavorings will turn out clear or lightly colored. That may prove disconcerting to some of your customers, who expect orange pop to be bright orange, cherry to be bright red. You might want to add a few drops of food coloring to your soft drinks to create eye appeal.

• Mock Cola

In Chapter 2 I said I'd give you a cola recipe. If you look back at the "secret" formula for colas given in that chapter, you'll realize that the major ingredients are lemon and vanilla. Try mixing those in equal amounts. Then add a few drops of red, green, and yellow food coloring to turn your cola brown. Taste test it beside the real thing to see if your sample sippers can tell the difference.

• Flavored Syrups

You may find that simply adding flavors to carbonated water becomes boring before long. If you'd like to make your soda more from scratch, consider making some flavored syrups from fruit or other ingredients. This will produce a soft drink with no artificial flavors.

• Lemon or Orange Syrup

Add the freshly squeezed juice from three oranges or five lemons to one cup of sugar in a saucepan. Use a grater to shred the peel of one orange or lemon into the mixture. Add one cup of water and boil gently for five minutes. Store this syrup in the refrigerator and add one or two teaspoons to each glass of carbonated water to create real orange or lemon pop.

• Chocolate Syrup

This recipe first appeared in *Good Housekeeping* magazine in 1921. Add 1¾ cup boiling water to three squares of unsweetened chocolate. Mix in two cups of sugar and 1/8 teaspoon salt. Boil five minutes. Add two teaspoons of vanilla. Add one or two teaspoons to carbonated water. How do you like chocolate soda?

• Other Syrups

Griffith's Universal Formulary, published in 1854, described syrups of orange, almond, Spirit of Aromatics (ginger, cloves, sassafras), Neroli (orange and orris root), jasmine, violets, and red roses. Anyone for red rose soda pop? It might be worth a try—rose *tea* has long been popular.

Soft-Drink Recipes

You've now read how to make your own soda pop, and, I hope, you've actually followed the recipes and created a bottle or glass or several. Now let's look at some ways to use soft drinks.

Of course, you *can* simply enjoy glugging down your favorite pop along with millions of other people every day. But you might want to follow some of the suggestions of Earl Shorris of the *San Francisco Chronicle* who has suggested that the drinking of soft drinks can be elevated to gourmet or connoisseur status. Satirizing some of the procedures followed by wine tasters, Shorris advises serving pop cold, but not ice cold: "Serious drinkers prefer their soda pop cold in the mouth, but not ice cold." The temperature of 42°F used in the Pepsi Challenge might be a good choice. Perhaps as a soft-drink gourmet you'll want to carry a small thermometer about with you.

To taste and appraise the flavor of a soda pop, Shorris suggests:

First, take a small sip into the mouth and hold it there; second, move the soda pop about in the mouth, letting it stream backward over the palate; third, swallow slowly, to feel the flavor all the way down the gullet.

137

To "clear the palate" between tastes of different soda drinks, he recommends that the soda popper "chew an ordinary chocolate bar."

• *Ice-Cream Soda*

The ice-cream soda is the basic spin-off treat using soft drinks. Pour a glass three quarters full with your favorite flavor, previously chilled. Add a scoop or two of ice cream that will blend in flavor. Popular combinations include:

- Root beer and vanilla ice cream (the root beer float)
- Club soda, chocolate syrup, and vanilla or chocolate ice cream (chocolate float)
- Ginger ale and sherbet
- Cola and vanilla ice cream
- 7-Up and just about any flavor ice cream

• *Ginger and Juice*

Mix up a batch of your favorite fruit juice—orange, grape, apple, grapefruit, lemonade—using ginger ale instead of water. Or try the same using club soda instead of ginger ale for a fizzier than usual fruit juice. Or mix freshly prepared juice (orange, lemon) with ginger ale.

• *Rosemary Sablack's Coca-Cola Cake*

In her *Cookbook for Teens* (available from the author, P. O. Box 83, Gulliver, Michigan 49840, $7.95), Rosemary Sablack suggests this recipe:

Ingredients:

1 (10 ounce) bottle Coca-Cola	2 cups flour
1 stick margarine (½ cup)	2 cups sugar
3 tablespoons cocoa	½ cup buttermilk (or ½ cup milk
½ cup vegetable oil	plus 1 tablespoon vinegar)
½ cup miniature marshmallows	2 eggs
1 teaspoon baking soda	1 teaspoon vanilla

1. Mix 1 cup Coca-Cola, margarine, cocoa, and vegetable oil in a sauce pan; bring to a boil.

2. Reserve remaining Coca-Cola for frosting.

3. Add marshmallows to hot mixture; stir until melted.

4. In a large bowl mix soda, flour, and sugar together.

5. Pour hot mixture over flour mixture; add buttermilk, eggs, and vanilla. Stir well by hand; do not use mixer.

6. Pour in a greased 13 × 9 cake pan.

7. Bake in a 350°F oven for 35 minutes or until a toothpick is clean after being inserted in center of cake.

Frosting:
   1 stick margarine (½ cup)
   2 tablespoons cocoa
   3 tablespoons Coca-Cola
   2½ cups powdered sugar
   ½ cup chopped walnuts, optional

1. In a small mixing bowl, combine all the above ingredients. Beat until creamy and smooth.

2. If too thick, add a few drops milk. If too thin add more powdered sugar.

3. Spread on cake.

• *Soda Pop Gelatin*

Explore the flavor effects of using a soft drink instead of water in flavored gelatin recipes. The Vernor's ginger ale company of Detroit suggests using one package each of lemon and lime gelatin, substituting Vernor's ginger ale for the water, and adding crushed pineapple, diced celery, maraschino cherries, and chopped nuts. The mixture is prepared according to the recipes on the gelatin package, turned into a gelatin mold, chilled, and flipped gently onto a plate to create a colorful gelatin salad. In addition to experimenting with different flavors—try salads made with lemon-line, orange soda, or root beer—you can vary salad ingredients, adding peaches, pears, apples, fruit cocktail, or mandarin oranges.

• Baked Apples

From the Vernor's kitchen comes the suggestion of baking apples in a soft drink, specifically, Vernor's ginger ale. Place six peeled and cored apples in a shallow pan. Pour in about ½ inch of Vernor's; sprinkle the apples with cinnamon; pour more Vernor's into the apple centers. Bake at 375°F for about forty-five minutes.

• Baked Ham

One last one from Vernor's (again a recipe that can be adapted to many of your favorite soft drinks): place a five-pound boneless *pre-cooked* ham in a shallow baking dish. Combine three tablespoons brown sugar with a little soda pop. Use this mixture to coat the ham. Cover with aluminum foil and bake at 350°F for 1½ hours. Uncover for the last fifteen minutes.

• Rusty Nut Knuckle Unbuster

If you have a nut that's stuck on your bicycle, before you bruise your knuckles trying to muscle it off with a wrench, coat the threads of the bolt as well as the nut itself with your favorite soft drink. Let it stand for several hours or overnight. With luck, the nut will turn easily, because the mild acid in most soft drinks will eat through the corrosion and free the joint.

APPENDIX

For Further Information— Addresses

Here is a list of the addresses of a number of major regional and national soft-drink brands. If the address of a company you want to reach isn't here, check the yellow or white pages of the phone book for the name of your local bottler or distributor. You'll also find directories of business addresses at your local library; ask the librarian for help. Address your correspondence to the Public Relations Department of the company.

The Coca-Cola Company
P. O. Drawer 1734
Atlanta, Georgia 30301

The Cola Clan
2084 Continental Drive N.E.
Atlanta, Georgia 30345

(The Cola Clan is a national
organization of collectors of
Coke memorabilia.)

Dr Pepper Company
5523 E. Mockingbird Lane
Dallas, Texas 75222

(Use the same address for Canada
Dry)

Faygo Beverages
3579 Gratiot
Detroit, Michigan 48207

141

Hires Company
c/o Procter & Gamble
P. O. Box 599
Cincinnati, Ohio

Moxie Industries
5775-B Peachtree
Dunwoody NE
Atlanta, Georgia 30342

National Soft Drink Association
1101 Sixteenth Street, Northwest
Washington, D.C. 20036

(Members of this organization
   include a great many soft-drink
   bottlers all over the country.)

Nehi Royal Crown Corporation
2801 West 47th Street
Chicago, Illinois 60638

PepsiCo, Inc.
Pepsi-Cola Company
Purchase, New York 10577

Shasta Beverages
26901 Industrial Blvd.
Hayward, California 94545

Seven-Up Company
121 S. Meramek
St. Louis, Missouri 63105

Vernors, Inc.
4501 Woodward Avenue
Detroit, Michigan 48201

Yoo-Hoo Chocolate Beverage
   Group
600 Commercial Avenue
Carlstadt, New Jersey 07072

Bibliography

In writing this book, I consulted several hundred sources, including books, magazines, and newspaper articles written from 1890 to the present. I also wrote to the archivists of several soft-drink companies and corresponded with soda poppers all over the country. To list the reference to every statement or quotation in this book would have cluttered each page with footnotes, many of them to sources that are hard to come by. The following books were major references in my study, and you can obtain most of them in libraries or by writing directly to the publisher.

The Coca-Cola Company: An Illustrated Profile. Atlanta: The Coca-Cola Company, 1974.

Lawrence Dietz. *Soda Pop: The History, Advertising, Art, and Memorabilia of Soft Drinks in America.* New York: Simon and Schuster, 1973.

Harry E. Ellis. *Dr Pepper: King of Beverages.* Dallas: The Dr Pepper Company, 1979. (Available from the publisher: 5523 E. Mockingbird Lane, Dallas, Texas 75222.)

Ron Fowler. *An Introduction to Collecting Soda Pop Bottles.* Seattle: Dolphin Point Writing Works, 4110-48th N.E., 1984. (Available from the author:

$4.95 plus $1 postage and handling. Washington residents add 39¢ sales tax.)

Milward W. Martin. *Twelve Full Ounces.* New York: Holt, Rinehart, and Winston, 1962.

Frank N. Potter. *The Moxie Mystique.* Newport News, Virginia: Published by the author, 1981. (Available from Frank N. Potter, 29 Franklin Road, Newport News, Virginia 23601. $6.95, including postage and handling.)

John J. Riley. *A History of the American Soft Drink Industry.* Washington, D.C.: American Bottlers of Carbonated Beverages, 1958.

Solveig Paulson Russell. *Peanuts, Popcorn, Ice Cream, Candy and Soda Pop.* Nashville: Abingdon Press, 1970.

Ira Shannon. *Brand Name Guide to Sugar.* Chicago: Nelson-Hall, 1977.

Pat Watters. *Coca-Cola: An Illustrated History.* Garden City: Doubleday, 1978.

John Yudkin. *Sweet and Dangerous.* New York: Peter H. Wyden. 1972.

For other books, check with your local library. You can also keep up on happenings in the soda-pop world by checking recent issues of the *Reader's Guide to Periodical Literature* at your library. Look under "Beverages—Carbonated" for articles about small and large skirmishes in the soda-pop wars.

Index

Acid stomach, 8
Addresses, manufacturers', 141-42
Advertising, 57-72
  celebrities, 66-70
  Coca-Cola, 60
  collectibles, 58, 59-61
  giveaways, 58
  Pepsi-Cola, 60
  slogans, 70-73
Alcohol, 76-78
Alka-Seltzer, 10
Anka, Paul, 68
Apples, baked (recipe), 140
Archer, Frank, 65
Armstrong, Frank, 96
Aspartame, 110 (see also Nutra-
  Sweet)
Aspen, origins, 102

Berra, Yogi, 55
Bottle capper, 125
Bottled water, 5
Bottles, 11-12

Coca-Cola, 60-62
Dr Pepper, 62
Moxie, 63-64
plastic, 98
sizes, 97
Bottling, franchise system, 29
Bradham, Caleb, 37-40
Byrd, Larry, 68

Caffeine, 26, 48, 51, 112-14
Calories, 105
Canada Dry, 21
  origins, 51-52
Candler, Asa, 27-30
Candler, Howard, 30-32
Cans,
  flat-top, 98
  pop-top, 98
  tin, 97
Caps,
  crown, 19
  resealable, 98
  twist-off, 98

145

Carbonation, 6, 7-10, 12, 124
Carbon dioxide, 7-9
Carcinogens, 108
Chero-Cola, 79
Chocolate syrup (recipe), 136
Claus, Santa, 69
Coca-Cola,
    "classic," 37
    cocaine rumors, 25, 75
    imitators, 35-37
    ingredients, 25, 30-33, 36, 37
    international sales, 81-82
    legend of, 25-27
    logotype, 27, 34
    mergers, 95
    "new," 37
    patents, 35, 39, 60-62
    secret recipe, 30-33, 36, 37
    war efforts, 78, 80-82
    (see also Rivalry)
Coca-Cola cake (recipe), 138-39
Cocaine, 25, 75
Coca leaves, 25
Cohan, George M., 67
Cola leaves, 112
Cola nut, 25
Cola nut bottle, 61
Consumption, soft-drink statistics,
    58, 90, 116-17
Conway, Tim, 68
Cosby, Bill, 68, 87-88
Crawford, Joan, 68
Crosby, Bing, 67
Crown cap, 19
Cyclamates, 107-08

Diet Coke (origins), 111
Diet Pepsi (origins), 108
Diet Rite (origins), 107-08
Diet soft drinks, 103-12, 116-17
Dorsett, Tony, 68

Dr Pepper, 21
    advertising, 90
    bottling, 48
    cures, 49
    international sales, 94
    logotypes, 49, 59
    merger, 52
    origins, 45-50
    patents, 47
    sugar in, 79-80
    war effort, 79-80

Eddy, Walter, 79-80
Ellis, Harry, 50
Erving, Julius, 68

Fahlberg, C. H., 106
Fanta (origins), 99
Faygo, 68
Ferraro, Geraldine, 70
Flavors,
    artificial, 15-18
    chemical, 16-17
    home use (recipes), 134
Food and Drug Administration (see
    Pure Food and Drugs)
Ford, Whitey, 55
Franchise system, 29, 30
Fresca (origins), 100
Fruit juice soda (recipe), 131

Ginger ale (recipe), 130 (see also
    Canada Dry)
Ginger and juice (recipe), 138
Ginger beer, 17
    recipe, 14
Gourmet soda poppers, 137
Greeks, 4
Greene, "Mean" Joe, 87-88
Grigg, C. L., 50-51
Guth, Charles, 39

Ham, baked (recipe), 140
Hawthorne, Nathaniel, 17
Health and health claims, 4, 5, 6,
    75-76, 105-06, 117
  Coca-Cola, 50
  Hires, 23-24
  Moxie, 41
  7-Up, 50
Herbs and herb drinks, 12, 129
  soft drink (recipe), 131
Hires, Charles, 22-24
Hires' Root Beer,
  advertising, 21-25
  bottling, 22-23
  health claims, 23-24
  home brewing, 22, 122
  ingredients, 22
  origins, 21-25
  sugar free, 110-11
Holmes, Oliver Wendell, 36
Howard, Elston, 55
Hydro-therapy, 4

Ice-cream soda (recipe), 138
International competition, 91-94

Jackson, Michael, 68-70
Jacob's Drug Store, 26
Johnson, "Magic," 68

Kent, Alan Bradley and Austen
    Herbert Croom, 73
Khrushchev, Nikita, 93

Lamarr, Hedy, 67
Lemon syrup (recipe), 135
Logotypes,
  Coca-Cola, 27
  Pepsi-Cola, 38
  Dr Pepper, 49, 50

Mantle, Mickey, 55
McLaughlin, John, 51-52
Mello Yello (origins), 100

Mock cola (recipe), 135
Mock root beer (recipe), 130
Mooney, Philip, 33-34
Morrison, Wade, 46-48
Mountain Dew (origins), 100
Moxie,
  bottle, 63
  bottling, 42
  giant bottle, 63-64
  health claims, 40-41
  imitators, 43
  meaning of, 43
  merger, 96
  outsells Coke, 66
Moxie man, 65-66
Moxiemobile, 65, 85
Mr. PiBB (origins), 100

New York Yankees, 55-56
Nixon, Richard, 93
No-cal pop, 106
Nutra-Sweet, 111, 117

Old Corner Drug Store, 47
Olivieri, Natale, 54-55
Orange syrup (recipe), 136

Packard, Vance, 89
Painter, William, 19
Pemberton, John, 25-27
Pepper, Dr. Kenneth, 46-47
Pepsi Challenge, 83-87
Pepsi-Cola,
  advertising, 68-70, 71, 72, 83-87
  jingle, 73
  logotype, 38
  mergers, 95
  origins, 37-40
  patents, 38
  sugar problems, 79-80
  (see also Rivalry)
Pepsi Free (origins), 114

Pepsi generation, 72, 73
Pepsi Light (origins), 100
Potter, Frank, 41, 43
Priestley, Joseph, 7-9
Prohibition, 76-78
Psychological appeals, 89, 91
Pure Food and Drugs, 17, 24, 44,
    49, 57, 74-76, 106, 109-10, 112
Pyrmont water, 5, 8

Ramblin' Root Beer (origins), 102
Ritchie, Lionel, 70
Rivalry, Coca-Cola vs. Pepsi-Cola,
    39-40, 83-84, 87-88, 91-94, 112
Rivers, Joan, 68
Robinson, Frank, 27, 29
Romans, 4
Root beer, 14, 17
    home-made, 121-22, 129
    recipe, 129
Root Glass Company, 61
Ross, Ken, 88
Royal Crown, 94, 107-08
    origins, 79
Rusty nut knuckle unbuster, 140

Saccharin, 106, 107, 109, 111
Saratoga Springs, 6
Schweppe, Jacob, 10
7-Up,
    cures, 51
    origins, 50-51
    uncola, 51, 114
Shorris, Earl, 137-38
Silliman, Benjamin, 11-12, 19
Skowron, Bill "Moose," 55
Skywriting, 71
Small beer, 13
Soda fountain, 17-19
Soda fountain pop (recipe), 133

Soda pop gelatin (recipe), 139-40
Sodium, 114-15
Sprite (origins), 99
Squirt, diet, 111
Sugar,
    health effects, 103-06
    industry, 108-09
    stockpiles, 78-79
Sveda, Michael, 107
Switchel, 13
Syrup,
    flavored (recipes), 135
    sugar (recipe), 133

TAB (origins), 108
Teem (origins), 180
Thompson, Augustin, 41-43, 45
Tittle, Y.A., 67
Tonic, 1

Un-cola, 51, 114

Venable, Willis, 26
Vernor, James, 53
Vernors Ginger Ale, 52-54, 139,
    140
Vichy water, 5, 6

Walnut cream (recipe), 135
Wars,
    soft-drink, 83-102
    world, 78-82
Washington, George, 6
White, William Allen, 78
Wiley, Harvey, 57, 74, 75, 77, 106,
    113
Woodruff, Robert, 80-81
Wynn, Ed, 66

Yoo-Hoo (origins), 54-55

91-359

338.4   Tchudi, Stephen N.
TCH
         Soda poppery

$13.95

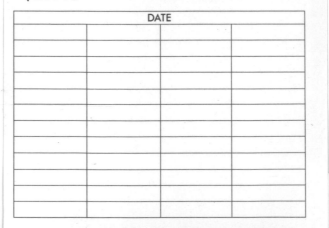

DATE		

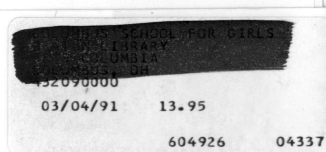